THE FARRIER'S SON

By

Michael T. Gmoser

The Farrier's Son By Michael T. Gmoser
Cover design by Jan Kostka, Image by William Steward
Wrong Way Books is an imprint of
Winged Hussar Publishing, LLC, 1525 Hulse Road, Unit 1, Point Pleasant, NJ 08742

This edition published in 2017 Copyright ©Winged Hussar Publishing, LLC

ISBN 978-1-950423-24-8 Paperback
ISBN 978-1-950423-68-2 Hardback
ISBN 978-1-950423-25-5 E-book
Library of Congress No. 2020935587
Bibliographical references and index
1.Mystery 2. Detective 3. Action & Adventure

Winged Hussar Publishing, LLC All rights reserved

For more information on Winged Hussar Publishing, LLC, visit us at: https://www.WingedHussarPublishing.com
Twitter: WingHusPubLLC
Facebook: Winged Hussar Publishing LLC

THE FARRIER'S SON

Chapter One

"**I** am expecting great things from you, Tallbridge. I think you have what it takes to be a success in this office. The job is yours, if you still want it and I need you to start today," the County prosecutor said.

Spencer Tallbridge had interviewed to become an assistant prosecutor with the Rutledge County Prosecutor's Office, but because of his background as a defense attorney, he did not expect such a warm reception or job offer. The interview process was extensive with background checks and an interview with the chief assistant prosecutor of the Criminal Division. Spencer made the misplaced assumption that no one would want a fox in the hen house, but he was surprised and wrong.

"Yes sir, you bet. I mean, I accept, and I am grateful for the opportunity."

"I like your name, Tallbridge. It sounds distinguished. You're tall – it benefits a commanding presence in the court room."

Spencer thought the prosecutor was talking as if he were buying a horse and would comment next on his teeth.

"And you have good teeth and a friendly smile."

Spencer was not disappointed. Hopefully, he thought, there would be more to this work than name and appearance, but apparently he had met Herald's physical qualifications. Beyond those, Spencer had a serious demeanor caused partially by bags under his eyes resulting from too many defense trials with no support staff in his other life as small town defense lawyer. He also needed reading glasses that he seldom used causing him to squint in conversations that gave him the appearance of someone who was deeper in thought than he was. Still, time and age were on his side at 28 years and he was in better shape than those around him that were better fed.

The Prosecutor, Dan Herald, was a living legend around Rutledge County. At seventy he still looked like he was in his sixties. He was an imposing figure – tall, thin, and a cross between an angry Abraham Lincoln and a movie star. He had a square jawed face that looked like it was chiseled out of granite. With dark hair and eyes to match, he compared well with the public perception of a prosecutor as one being serious and no nonsense. He got his start in 1982 as an assistant prosecutor and within a year was handling his first of many death penalty cases. He never lost. He was generally considered to be a lawyer's lawyer and worthy of emulation, but not someone that would be invited out for a beer after hours.

"I will do my best, sir. You cut a wide path; I'll follow your lead."

Spencer was in awe of this legend. Herald was the sole reason he decided to take a shot at being an assistant prosecutor. He wanted to know from the inside how he did it. Just what was the secret to never losing a case? It had to be more than luck. After all, prosecutors do not make the facts. One way or another, facts find the prosecutors and not the other way around. Of course, Spencer thought, maybe Herald was just cherry-picking cases and able to pass off the tough ones, but that conclusion was not supported by his record. His best and most experienced attorneys were death penalty qualified and even among that group, Herald was considered the best of the best. Ultimately, it was Herald that could not pass those cases on to others.

"I am going to have the Chief show you around today and I have to get you sworn in. There are a few other details. I need you to sign a confidentiality oath. What is said here stays here. I don't want to hear something on the street that was private to this office and that it came from you. You will also get LEADS authorization for checking criminal histories and that's going to require you to be fingerprinted. I know you were printed when you applied to take the Bar examination, but that doesn't count. Are you familiar with LEADS?"

"Not really. I always got criminal histories from the prosecutors when I was on the other side and assumed it was some type of computerized records check, but I have never operated the system."

"Arnold will fill you in on that, but LEADS stands for Law Enforcement Automated Data System. I don't know who thinks up those acronyms, but it fits. Just remember this. If you use it to check on a friend, girlfriend or something personal, it's a felony and the system is audited; so be careful. When you get fingerprinted, you will also do a Buccal swab for DNA. I want you in that data base like the rest of us in case you ever touch something at a crime scene, and we need to know that you are not some mystery person. The prints are easy. The days of the ink and roll are history. You will just put your fingers on a screen, a button is pushed and that's it. Sort of like a copy machine except cleaner and quicker."

The Chief he referred to was Bill Arnold who was the head of the felony division to which Spencer was assigned. They met during the interview process. He had been with Herald almost from his start and was looking for retirement. For Herald, Arnold was the go-to guy and had a presence near equal to Herald. He was short, balding and looked more like an accountant than a lawyer with a well-earned reputation for detail. He saw his role as a watchdog over his division and he was responsible for annual performance evaluations. That alone gave him more power than any assistant in the office and why he always wanted to be addressed as Mr. Arnold by those in his charge. Arnold told Spencer that unlike a new hire fresh out of law school, he would not receive any specialized training. It was understood that Spencer knew the job from fighting against it and that Arnold would hear about any deficiencies from his many sources including judges and colleagues in the office.

"But before I turn you loose," Herald admonished, "I want to impress upon you how we do things here. Never forget you represent me, not just this office. What you do reflects on me personally, and I do not like to look bad. It's bad politics, too. If you want to sleep good at night after sending the bad guys to prison and listening to the wail of their families, remember we do justice first and winning cases is always second. It might be a close second, but winning it is always second. When winning is first you are likely to – no – you will do something stupid and, if you have a conscience, you will not sleep well. Get the point?"

"Yes, sir, I get it."

"I know you are going to screw up. I know you are going to make mistakes. I will be waiting to hear about you. When that day comes, tell me the truth. No bullshit. Don't lie. I will know and you will be fired. There're no secrets around here. Now on that happy note, let's get you sworn in."

For Spencer, it was not a happy note and it was not expected to be one. The seriousness of the moment came over Spencer like a cold wind that Herald knew would stay with him as he rose to signal that the meeting was over.

"Let me round up Arnold and he can take you down and get you sworn in," Herald said as he called out for his secretary to find him. "Just hang out for a while until he gets here. You won't be disappointed with him as my number one. Arnold runs the show. Got a question, he's your go-to guy. Got a problem, same. You probably already figured that out when he interviewed you," Herald said as he offered a firm congratulatory handshake and slowly closed his office door, leaving Spencer standing outside waiting for the next installment of his new career. It was a new job on a new day in early April with spring also on its way. For Spencer everything about that day was new and filled with hope for the future as long as he kept his nose clean and did his job.

The prosecutor's secretary, Ann Truster, was a few steps away and gave Spencer a disarming smile. She was the most pleasant and disarming person Spencer had met in the office and was the first to make him feel the warmth of a not so friendly place.

"Have a seat and welcome aboard. Mr. Arnold is on his way. I hope you will like your new job. Probably didn't expect to start today. Have you got a place to stay?"

"Actually, yes. Come hell or high water I was moving here. I needed a change. If I didn't meet you on this end, I would have eventually met you one way or the other. I rented an apartment down on Morris Avenue close to town."

"You come from a defense attorney background and we don't get a lot of those around here. At least not the experienced ones. What made you leave the dark side?" she asked with a muted laugh.

"Well, it's a long story," Spencer began with all the prosecutorial correctness he could muster, "but the short story is I simply got tired of representing guilty people and I hate to lose. In fact, I hate losing more than I like winning. I have a hard time getting over a loss and when you represent criminals, you lose a lot. All told, I would rather represent the interest of an innocent victim than the interest of a guilty criminal." Telling her that he still retained a remnant of youthful legal idealism in the system seemed too much to describe or probably for her to accept.

"Not as much money in that either, is there?" Ann said with a cynical laugh.

"We can agree on that. What idiot said crime pays?" Spencer said, as Arnold walked up on the conversation.

"How's it going, kid? Good to see you again," was his standard question and greeting. Without time for a reply Arnold said, "Let's get going. We have a lot of ground to cover. I want to get you sworn in and take you over to the Grand Jury to monitor those proceedings. After that you and I will have a sit down to set up your case load, get you squared away with a secretary, introduce you to the investigators, and pair you with a room assistant prosecutor to keep an eye on you. Sorry to sound so invasive, but it's the way we do things here. You know – it's the 'trust-but-verify' thing."

The prosecutor's office and all court-associated offices – probation, indigent services, and court rooms – were all located in the same complex. The prosecutor's office was located on the top floor of the ten-story building with all the courts located on the first and second floors for public convenience. The building was constructed with typical governmental efficiency for a county on a budget – short on design and tall on utility.

"You know, kid, I learned a lot about you from your inter-view," Arnold began. "The boss said you are a winner where you came from. He checked you out, too. I hear the prosecutor there is happy to get you out of his hair. I really don't think you will find prosecution much different than defense work. You obvi-ously have seen both sides and know the drill as we discussed."

Spencer listened and took it all in but wondered if Arnold really knew his first name. He never came off calling him "kid" and Spencer was not about to inquire. "We are going to Judge Macintosh. He's a crusty old Irishman and knows his stuff. He doesn't suffer fools well and I am not going to pair you with him. No offense."

"None taken." Spencer knew that a new hire is always a problem for a Judge and there was no need to look for trouble, if it could be avoided. Spencer just put his trust in Arnold to make a good fit.

The elevator opened on the second floor where the courtroom and chambers of Judge Macintosh were located. Along the corri-dor to the courtroom door there was a line of chairs with only an elderly disheveled gray-haired lady sitting and staring at the two as they approached.

Suddenly, as if she awoke from a daydream, she shouted, "Murderers, you're all murderers!" and repeated the phrase sev-eral times as they passed by.

"What the hell was that all about?" Spencer asked. He had not even been sworn in and he was already hated by at least one person in the building that he didn't even know.

"Well, you just met Molly," Arnold said. "There is a lot of history with her and you will just have to put up with it. She blames the boss and all of us for her son being on death row. Eventually she will give up or just die, but in the meantime the Judges let her rant whenever she gets a chance. It might be a free speech thing or maybe just their way of pissing off the boss."

"I hate to sound heartless, but there ought to be something that can be done about her. What if a prospective juror in the hall hears her as I'm walking into to a trial?" Spencer asked.

"I think we better have a little talk now," Arnold said.

As Arnold and Spencer walked down the hallway, Arnold stopped at the door of an attorney/client conference room that was in use. He entered without hesitation or a courteous knock on the door.

"Hello, Brady," Arnold said, interrupting the attorney talking with his client. Hope you don't mind, but I need this for a while."

"No problem, Mr. Arnold." Brady agreed also without hesitation.

Spencer was impressed with the command Arnold had over the appropriation. He took it as another learning experience that the Courthouse pecking order extended well beyond the office of the Prosecutor. Arnold shut the door and began with a history lesson he wanted Spencer to understand concerning the office and Molly.

"What I'm about to tell you stays here." Spencer nodded in agreement. "Years ago," Arnold continued, "the McBride murder case was a sensation. It shot Herald into office like being shot from a Howitzer and McBride's mother never got over the conviction. She has been nothing but trouble ever since and cost one of our assistant prosecutors his job and probably his life."

"You're not saying that Molly…?" Spencer began but was interrupted by Arnold.

"No. Of course not, but she sure as hell got him fired and he had a hard time with that. Being an assistant was his life. It was who he was, and he couldn't take being fired. He wasn't heartless either and bought into Molly's shtick."

"What's a 'shtick'?" Spencer asked.

"It's bullshit. Molly's well-rehearsed bullshit that her son was innocent. Around the same time DNA was just coming out as the be-all and end-all of innocence claims."

"So, what happened?" Spencer asked.

"The assistant prosecutor, Glenn Howard was his name, bought into it and took it upon himself to contact defense attorneys and gin up the idea that DNA in the McBride case was never properly handled or tested. We never saw it coming. Eventually, Herald found out like he always does and all hell broke loose. Before long, motions started flying around like a windstorm and McBride's execution was put on hold until it all got sorted out. In the end, the result was the same. McBride was guilty and Howard got fired. He took it hard, as I said, and started running his mouth about new evidence and that McBride was railroaded by the detectives. He claimed Herald knew Linda Stewart, too, like a lot of folks in town, and that the evidence against McBride was no stronger against him than a case would be against Herald, except, of course, McBride's confession. Making that comparison really pissed Herald off, as you might expect. Ultimately, no one believed him or took him seriously, except Molly, and he killed himself."

"How did he do it?"

"Bullet to the head," Arnold said. "He used a pistol found near his hand and it was traced back to one of his closed cases. It all fit."

"Was there a note?"

"No note; just dead. Herald had the coroner go through his apartment looking for one and recovered all his papers and computer stuff. The coroner gave it all to Herald. I think Herald looked for anything that might give a motivation beyond being fired, and I think Herald took it hard, too. I think he felt responsible, but who knew that Howard was as off balance as Molly. So, there it is. Don't let Molly get in your head. It's safer that way."

"Has anyone from our office ever reached out to Molly to explain the evidence of guilt and convince her that she is going down the wrong road?" Spencer asked. "Seems like the compassionate thing to do."

"We don't do compassionate explanations with the families of murderers."

"O.K, but at least it seems like the humane thing to do, and just maybe put an end to what I will have to deal with," Spencer said.

"We don't do humane either. We do prosecutions. That's as much as you need to know. Just keep Molly out of your head and take a lesson from Howard. Let's get back to business." Arnold signaled with that comment that the history lesson was over, and they gave the room back to Brady and his waiting client.

Spencer and Arnold entered the courtroom of Judge Macintosh and were greeted by his bailiff, Chuck Smith. Smith was a retired detective and a former Marine pilot from the Viet Nam era. He looked the part of both with his barreled chest and crew cut that he kept "high and tight" as he referred to it. His old military uniform would probably no longer fit and he tugged at his tie as if he was not comfortable with it, but Smith always gave his shoes a standard and recognizable military polish. He served multiple purposes for the judge including protection, running the courtroom recording system, and serving as the judge's political operative for reelection. For him the best part was playing chauffer and the judge's personal pilot that required him to stay fit to maintain his pilot license. Overall, his title was Bailiff. Like the judge, he was a no-nonsense type and knew how to move things along.

"What brings you down, Bill?" he asked with a smile that seemed to signal that he knew Arnold had a new assistant in tow.

"Well, we need to see the Judge to get this kid sworn in. This is…" Arnold hesitated for just a second and said, "…new hire Spencer Tallbridge, so I am hoping the Judge might be available."

Spencer felt like he finally had a name with Arnold and reached out to shake Smith's hand.

"Glad to meet you, Tollbridge. I think I can arrange a swearing in."

"It's Tallbridge – no toll to it," Spencer said with a smile as he felt Smith's firm military, police, and political handshake letting Spencer know who was in charge of the courtroom.

"At ease, gentlemen," Smith ordered as he knocked on the judge's chambers door, entered, and disappeared. It wasn't long before Judge Macintosh came out unceremoniously and appeared as advertised.

"So, you need to be sworn in and we can get that done. Bill, do you have the oath?" Spencer was relieved that there was no "let's get to know the assistant prosecutor" conversation. It was strictly business. The judge did not waste any time in getting on with the task at hand.

Arnold pulled the oath from his coat pocket and handed it to the Judge.

"OK, repeat after me," the judge began. For Spencer the oath was a meaningful moment and not just an essential requirement. He always thought that he lived the meaning of the oath anyway when he passed the Bar exam requiring no new promise to it. It did serve as a serious reminder of how he would continue to think and act with a promise to a higher authority.

"I, Spencer Tallbridge, do solemnly promise and swear that I will support the Constitution of the United States and the Constitution and laws of the State of Ohio and that I will faithfully perform and discharge all of the duties of an Assistant Prosecutor of the Prosecuting Attorney in Rutledge County, Ohio, to which I have been chosen, and to do justice in all things appurtenant to my position without respect to persons or property to the best of my ability and understanding, and this I do as I shall answer unto God. I further promise and swear to keep confidential any information which should come before me in the performance of the duties entrusted to me, so help me God."

"Congratulations," the judge said and asked to whose court room he would be assigned.

"Not sure yet," Arnold broke in, "but we are working on it."

Spencer thought that was not entirely true because he was already told he would not be the room prosecutor for Judge Macintosh.

Chapter Two

Following the meeting with Judge Macintosh, Spencer and Arnold went to Arnold's office to talk about duties, scheduling, and court room assignments and, as Arnold put it, "the rules of the road".

"I am pairing you with Judge Harris. He's a compassionate guy and sound in the law. He will expect you to know the law, but he's not as tough on assistants as some of the others. His Grand Jury cases are being presented this afternoon and his current room prosecutor is Joe Salyers. I will turn you over to Joe when we go down to the Grand Jury. You won't have your own secretary. You have to share one, but Amy is really good and has been here a long time. Your office is next to hers so it should be easy for her to show you the ropes, if needed."

"What can I expect as a case load?" Spencer asked.

"Well, it's usually around twenty cases a month. I want you to apply the FBI approach as best you can."

"FBI approach? What is the FBI approach?"

Arnold hesitated for a moment to collect his explanation. "The FBI does not take crap shoots. It does not have the time or resources to take on close cases. If it's not perfect, if a conviction is not guaranteed, the case does not see the light of day and disappears off the radar. We may not be perfect, but close. Get the picture?"

"Got it," Spencer said.

Arnold went on to tell Spencer about how he would be monitored. Joe Salyers would be required to do a monthly evaluation for the first six months before Spencer was fully on his own. Joe could make him or break him was the message, so it would pay to be on his good side and do a good job. Arnold's last instruction was a word of caution.

"I know you're a single guy and we have a good-looking staff, but there is a 'No Fraternization' rule here which the boss strictly enforces. In other words, don't dip your pen in company ink."

"No problem," Spencer responded. "I get the point."

"We will meet at the Grand Jury at 1:30 p.m. You know where it is?" Arnold asked as if he expected Spencer would know.

"Not really, no. But I'll...."

"Third Floor, can't miss it, but let's get you situated in your new office and introduce you to Joe and his secretary, Amy Jacobs. I think you will also get along with her. Amy gets along with everyone. Seems to be her nature. She will also have more paperwork for you – tax information – all the business stuff to get you started. I think Joe's in his office, and I'll walk you over."

As Spencer and Arnold traversed the expansive office floor of the prosecutor's office, Spencer sensed that the entire office staff was on alert to the new hire on deck. There were occasional glances by the secretarial staff and assistant prosecutors were coincidentally standing in their office doors pouring over briefs and documents, but he knew he was on stage. He was the new guy and would be tested sooner or later. Every assistant prosecutor he ever went against had a competitive gene and it would make no difference that he was now on the same side. Finally, they arrived at the office of Joe Salyers, who was also standing in his doorway seemingly engrossed in a case file.

"Salyers, I want you to meet Spencer," Arnold said. He hesitated a moment and said, "Tallbridge. Herald just hired him, and he starts today in the felony division. He has an interesting background that just might give you guys some perspective. He is now, happily, a former defense attorney from over in Wooster and was a real pain in the ass to the prosecutor there. I want you to fill him in on the staff and I need him at 1:30 for your Grand Jury. Should be a good opportunity to see how we work it here," he said walking away.

"No problem, Mr. Arnold," Salyers said. "Nice to meet you, Spencer. Have a seat. I suppose Herald gave you his 'we do justice first' speech."

"Yes, and a lot more, especially about the 'pen in company ink' thing."

"Well, yes. That was a problem for a while, but not anymore after a secretary got knocked up by an assistant prosecutor. It was kind of funny for a while until she had triplets. Then it got really serious. It can happen anywhere I guess, and Herald does not want it to happen again. The crime we have here is no different than anywhere else. You will get tired of the drug cases and drug defenses. You already know how creative defense attorneys are with motions to suppress evidence. Eighty-five percent of all the cases we handle have some element of drug abuse or that drugs are a motivating factor. Those are the ones that come to you looking for a break. It used to be that the 'devil made me do it' or 'demon rum made me do it'. Now, it's just 'drugs made me do it'. You'll have to get past that and just do your job and not get into the mitigation thing. I just let the judges do that."

"How does plea bargaining play into that? I mean do we take into consideration the use of drugs in working out pleas?"

"Maybe you were able to do that over in Wooster, but we don't here. Herald likes to be consistent and that is hard to do when we add non-defenses to mitigation as defenses for plea bargaining. Does that make sense? What I want you to consider is asking me for a while anyway to keep you out of trouble with Arnold. He will be watching you, but don't get too self-conscious about it."

"That might be hard to do. Thanks for letting me pick your brain on that stuff. Do you have any idea of what's in the pipeline for me? I mean anything real serious that I need to prepare for?"

"Did Arnold tell you about a case that came back from the Supremes?"

Salyers was referring to a felonious assault conviction that was recently reversed by the Ohio Supreme Court and would have to be retried with the clock ticking to get it done.

"No, he didn't mention it. What's going on?"

"Don't mention I told you, but you're the new guy and shit falls downhill. It's the Compton case and the conviction got reversed. The assistant who tried it quit, and it has to be retried in a few months. No one, meaning me as the room prosecutor for Judge Harris, wants it. It has problems and new guys get the problems. Sorry. I thought I would tell you now, so you won't hold it against me later when you get the assignment."

"Looks like I'm being set up for a loss," Spencer responded.

"You are," Salyers said, "but don't worry about it. Nobody expects you to win any way. The victim got her head bashed in and can't remember anything. Once you get assigned, I'll go over it with you and help you out as much as I can with what's left. There was some pretty good evidence that isn't so good now after the Supremes got done with it. Bad luck. The good luck is you won't have a death penalty case here, if that's what you mean about what might also be on your plate. Those are the private preserve of the boss. He made his bones on one when he started and never looked back and never shared one either."

"You mean he never has an assistant with him?"

"Never," Salyers said emphatically.

"Do you at least have a committee to decide which cases he goes after death?"

"Nope, it's all on him and it's his baby. We just stay out of it. All things considered, none of us really care. Not my decision and not my problem when he pulls the trigger. What the hell, the defense wins 25% of all death penalty cases with a 'not guilty' anyway and the few that get it carried out deserve it."

"I never heard that the defense wins acquittals in 25%. That seems a little high from my experience over in Wooster."

"Thought you might ask. Every death penalty case gets appealed over and over. Delay is the first line of defense as you know. It's the defense strategy. As you also know those take years and 25% of all defendants condemned to death die of natural causes while waiting on the appeals process."

"I think I get it," Spencer said. "So, if a defendant dies while waiting on an appeal, the case is dismissed and there is no guilty finding. That's remarkable."

"You got it. Most people never figure that one out. Probably don't care and it is virtually impossible for anyone 70 or older to live long enough to be executed in this country. I always thought that might be a good equal protection argument if I were on the other side, but our appellate section says that's a non-starter. I won't even ask what your feelings are about the death penalty, but I recommend you keep them to yourself around here especially if you disagree that the penalty is a deterrent. The boss is big on that. Whatever your thoughts, it won't change anything around here and you don't want to get on the wrong side of that argument with the boss."

"I met Murder Molly today. I'm an hour into this job walking down the hall with Arnold and she calls me a murderer. How did she figure out who I was?"

"Guilt by association, young man. If you're with Arnold, you're one of us in her demented mind. You just have to get used to her. Some folks just don't have anything better to do and the courthouse is a great place to see all life's problems in action. It's a free show. She just happens to be fixated on one, and only one, and that will be over in a few months. By the way, it's always Mr. Arnold. He's kind of sensitive about it. It's the 'he's one of us, but one step above' thing, if you know what I mean."

"Right. I'll try to remember. Were you around when Molly's son went on trial?"

"No. It was way before my time. Arnold was here. I think he started about the same time the boss started. I heard through the vine that Arnold wanted the job, but Herald took on Molly's son's case, won it, and never looked back at any competition. Some of the stories are legendary and I suppose you have heard about those."

"I heard he never lost a death penalty case and he's working on that 75%," calling attention to the number of those who do not die of natural causes while waiting to be executed.

"That's right, but that will probably change. It is getting harder and harder to kill someone when the jury is given the opportunity to vote for life without the possibility of parole and there doesn't seem to be any limit on defense creativity in concocting mitigating factors for jury consideration. The only things they don't get to use are violins," he said laughing. "I assume you're not married."

"What make you say that?"

"No ring."

"Ordinarily that would be a good assumption, but better as an inference," Spencer said, drawing a legal distinction about proof. "You are right though. I'm not married and haven't been. Not that I'm opposed to it. I don't wear rings in any event because of a bad experience during a summer factory job. I worked in a shipping department for a farm parts supplier and on the first day our boss showed us college kids a photograph of what happens when you get a ring caught on a parts bin while falling. It was a picture, several actually, of a ring finger that was ripped entirely off an arm with foot-long tendons and muscles still attached. Now that was a life lesson I will never forget, and I will never wear a ring no matter what."

"Never thought of that. Makes sense and good point on assumptions. I should have known better. Could have been a religious thing, too."

Spencer realized that Salyers was getting to know him and perhaps not just for his benefit. It was Arnold's way of learning about him and Salyers was tagged with that extra duty.

"No. Not a religious thing. I'm not very religious and whatever I have, I don't wear it on my shirt sleeves."

Salyers seemed satisfied and there were no more inquiries about his private life at least for now. Salyers continued with an overview of the office operation and what was expected of him. If he lost a case, he could expect a review panel to give the case a postmortem led by Arnold. The idea was not to lose cases and thus avoid the inquisition to follow from peer review.

"I don't want to alarm you, but we are basically people processors. Someone is charged and we process to a conclusion. How well we do that determines how long we get to be employed and how much we get paid."

"Does Herald show any signs of slowing down? He seems he has overstayed usual retirement."

"I don't think so and no one talks about it. That might be a dangerous thing to do. I mean not physically, but if he ever thinks you are a candidate for his job, well, hasta la vista, baby. I think we better shove off for the Grand Jury. Arnold is probably already there and wants to cycle you into the process, if you know what I mean."

"Yeah, I get it. Let's go," and as they left Salyers introduced Spencer to their joint secretary, Amy Jacobs, who would also help Spencer to stay on track with the daily grind. She knew the business end of the work the assistant prosecutors do. Essentially, she put in words and onto paper the necessary court filings that were required before, during and after each case was completed. A misstep in that process might require days, weeks or even months to correct. Attention to detail was her hallmark and a blessing to those she worked with directly.

"Amy, this is the new guy, Spencer Tallbridge, and you will be working with him along with me. We're going down to the Grand Jury and will be back in a few."

"Hello, Amy. I look forward to working with you," Spencer said.

Accommodatingly, Amy said, "I look forward to working for you, too, Mr. Tallbridge."

"'Spencer' works for me. OK?" Spencer said, clarifying their first name basis going forward.

As she gratefully acknowledged the informality of their future relationship, Spencer and Salyers left and made their way to the Grand Jury where Arnold was already waiting and ready to proceed.

"Let's get started," Arnold said without further instructions to Spencer and all three entered the inner sanctum sanctorum of the Grand Jury chamber, shrouded in secrecy where Spencer had never been before. Arnold began with a brief introduction and made it clear to all in attendance that the Grand Jury did not indict "ham sandwiches", as a metaphor for a bad case often reported cynically by television pundits.

"Indict a ham sandwich and you will have to eat it," Arnold said sternly. "All officer-involved shootings will come to you. No exceptions. My boss will never independently determine that any such case is a justifiable homicide. You decide that."

At that point a hand went up from a Grand Juror and asked why?

"Good question," Arnold answered. "Let's say it's an easy one that anyone might think is justifiable and my boss says it's justifiable. OK. No problem. Then along comes one that is really politically charged and there is a public outcry for a Grand Jury determination, and it is sent up to you. Just what does that say? They may have been identical cases on the facts, but now the public sees one going to the Grand Jury. That tells the public that the one that goes up must have something criminal to it and that is not fair to the jury pool or the public."

It was an insightful moment that was not lost on all in attendance and routine for Arnold, who had told the same story for years; he enjoyed the total look of understanding and agreement on their faces. Next, he implored them not to indict on cases that could never be proved beyond a reasonable doubt, even if there were a probability that a crime was committed, and a person or persons probably committed it. Spencer was impressed with Arnold's narration of the duties of the Grand Jury as Arnold saw those and saw firsthand that prosecutors were not just all about winning an indictment because, in the final analysis, an indictment means nothing regarding proof of a crime. While that may seldom be acknowledged at a trial, there was efficiency and justice in making the point to the Grand Jury that bad cases are a waste of time.

"Will we hear a death penalty case?" a juror asked. "Before we got here and were being selected by the Judge to sit as members of the Grand Jury, she didn't know of any pending death penalty cases and she was only concerned if we could follow the law. She told us you would tell us what the laws are that apply to the evidence and we get that from you. Is that really it, more or less?"

"More or less that's right and I don't know of any case now pending, I mean coming up, that carries the death penalty.

If there ever is one, however, you will meet my boss, Prosecutor Herald, who has always handled those personally. As Prosecutor, he feels a special obligation to the public to handle those himself and it's quite a show. Well, not really a show, but as dramatic as those cases can be and with his talent for persuasion, those cases can seem like a show. In the meantime, assistants like Mr. Salyers here and our new hire here will give all you need to make good and honest decisions that will let you sleep well at night."

Arnold droned on for another 20 minutes telling the jury about the application of the Grand Jury to the Constitution and need for total secrecy of the proceedings before turning it over to Salyers to present the first case. Spencer took it all in as the cases were called and felt confident that he had made a good career change in going over to the right side of the scales of justice or as he often now referred to it as the "light side of justice".

At the end of the day, Salyers asked Spencer if he wanted to meet some of the staff after hours.

"You want to meet at AB's tonight?"

"Who's Abe?" Spencer asked.

"It's not a person; it's a cop bar called *Alibis*. We call it AB's for short and the general public doesn't know what we're talking about when we're going to a bar. The joke is that if a cop gets in trouble, he can always say he has an alibi. Get it?" he said laughing.

"Sure. Where is it? You know I don't know much about this town yet. Probably a good idea to get to know some of the men in blue."

"Straight down Tenth Street from the parking lot at the corner of Tenth and Maple. I'll see you there."

Chapter Three

Spencer made his way to Alibis and looked forward to the opportunity to hoist a few beers with the men he considered to be the good guys. It was a corner neighborhood bar and run by a former-now-retired police detective sergeant named Finnegan. As Irish as he was with his Irish temperament, he managed to handle rowdy patrons diplomatically and was a friend to anyone willing to listen to his exploits as a detective and crime fighter. It was a friendly place and most all the patrons knew each other from the force. To Spencer, it seemed to be as close as anyone could come to being in a bar like Cheers on the television program from his childhood. What Spencer liked about it most was the low, muted conversations throughout and no loud music that disrupted normal thought processes in more modern venues. While he still considered himself to be a young man, he felt he was too old for those places and welcomed the new associations he hoped to make that night. As he walked in, Salyers called out to him.

"Hey, Spencer. I'm over here. I want you to meet someone."

Spencer made his way to the far end of the bar to a table with Salyers and two uniformed off-duty patrol officers.

"Spencer, I want you to meet Officer Duffy and Officer Petty. And gentlemen, this is Spencer Tallbridge, a new felony assistant in our office. We broke him in today so I think he could use a beer," as he called out to Finnegan to bring over a bottle of Bud.

Petty was the first to speak. "So, tell me, Spencer, how do you feel about police work?" getting right to the point of their new association with him.

"I like it fine," he responded, "but I'll like it a whole lot better if they're paying for the beer." Spencer had not received his first pay check from his new role as an assistant prosecutor and his small savings as a former starving defense lawyer were wearing thin.

"I like this guy," Duffy said. "He gets right to the point of the important stuff."

From there everyone at the table took a more relaxed tone and talked about the police and prosecution problems of the day.

"Salyers tells us before you got here that you worked the other side," Duffy commented.

"I did. Didn't like it much. Finally decided to work on the light side. You know the one that doesn't work in the dark like the defense."

"Not sure if I follow. I get the light part, but what was dark on the other side?" Duffy asked.

"When you represent a defendant you never really know where the truth is. You can't rely on your client to be truthful. They usually don't tell the truth even when they're on surveillance video. That's why I call it the dark side. Maybe I'm just jaded about the defense and needed a change. Really, I'm lucky to get this job and from what I've seen so far you guys do a lot of justice around here."

"We think so," Salyers added with Duffy and Petty nodding in agreement.

"The only thing that has bothered me so far is Murder Molly and…"

The two officers broke into a laugh interrupting what Spencer was about to tell them and what they already knew.

"Molly's been around calling all of us murderers for years," Petty said. "You can't let her get under your skin. If she does, you lose and that's not smart. I think I speak for all of us on the department when I say I genuinely feel sorry for her, but I want her son to rot in hell. We have a county and a prosecutor where you can count on that. There is just no arguing with Molly. Many have tried and I'm surprised that she hasn't gotten herself committed. Just the same, in about six months McBride gets what's coming to him and that will be the end of it."

"Well said, my well-spoken friend," Duffy replied. "Once it's over I doubt we will see much more of Molly. It probably will kill her one way or another. Hard not to feel sorry for her though. I can't imagine what it's like having a son on death row all these years. Not much of a life for either one when you stop to think about it."

Spencer observed that no one seemed to give much thought to the execution beyond the occasional disruption caused by Molly, and that was about to change.

"How do you feel about the death penalty, Spencer?" Salyers asked.

By then Spencer had had a few beers and lost some of his concern that Salyers was measuring him up for Arnold or Herald. Salyers had told him to be cautious on the subject, but with three purported allies at the table and an invitation from his mentor to pontificate, Spencer decided to dive into the issue that has been argued constantly across the entire nation with every execution and that no harm would come to him from doing so.

"That's a damn good question and fortunately one I probably will never have to answer publicly," Spencer responded. "From what I learned today, death cases are the private preserve of Prosecutor Herald and no one else will ever find out what it's really like to try one as long as he's Prosecutor. But do I agree with it? I've seen it from both sides. Maybe three sides and maybe four or more sides. It seems like every year more sides are added to the argument."

"OK," Finnegan responded. "Where are the sides as you see it?" Duffy asked.

"On one side," Spencer continued, "it costs everyone a hell of a lot of time and money to try one and you might not live long enough to see the end result. It does beg the question just what did we get out of that. On another side, the times are a-changing, like the folk song and some day it will just end after all the time and expense. I would not want to be the guy that got the needle the day before that happened. Talk about your bad luck, but it will happen to some unlucky killer. On another side, there are those that are exonerated years later and a few, never mentioned, that get exonerated long after we execute them."

"Do you really think that anyone has ever been executed that didn't deserve it?" Petty asked.

"I'm not sure," Spencer admitted. "I heard about a case in Georgia a long time ago. It was a case about a factory superintendent named Leo Frank who was convicted of raping and murdering a young girl and he was sentenced to death, but after his appeals failed, the governor commuted his sentence because of problems he saw with the trial.

"So he wasn't executed after all and the justice system worked, right?" Petty asked.

"He was executed, but not by the State of Georgia and I guess you could say the system didn't work. After the governor commuted his sentence, a mob broke into the prison, kidnapped him and then lynched him by hanging him from a tree. It all happened in the early 1900s and I think some type of investigation later cleared Frank of the rape and murder, but we'll never know for sure. He might have been guilty and justice took a back seat to vengeance. I do think about that, but overall, I think the death penalty has been at least correctly applied to valid convictions. I mean valid within the rules of evidence, but for me that's more belief than fact. I don't know of any case where an innocent person has been lawfully executed by state action, but it is possible and odds are, it has happened."

"What side are you on? You don't have a problem with it do you?" Duffy asked.

Finnegan was now leaning in on the conversation and was anxious to here where the new assistant prosecutor stood after all the years of success with death penalty cases his detectives had with Herald. Like the others, he was trained to be a good listener and Spencer felt that he was now the oracle of truth to those in attendance.

"The problem I have always had with the death penalty comes out of my legal background," Spencer explained. "We lawyers are trained in the Constitution and are supposed to zealously protect equal protection under the law. Of course you know that there is a federal death penalty. McVey is the perfect example. He's that Oklahoma bomber who killed hundreds and federal law applies equally across the entire nation independently of state boundaries. Now the states do it differently because of state rights. A guy kills in New York and can at best get life, but a guy kills in Ohio and he can get death."

"But the states themselves are different so their laws are different," Salyers interjected.

"The people in New York like their jeans and burgers just the same as we do and the idea that a border makes a difference in these times no longer makes sense," Spencer argued.

"OK," Finnegan responded. "Where are you after putting all that legal mumbo jumbo aside?"

"I'm an eye for an eye guy," Spencer stated. "Politicians and prosecutors sell that as advocating deterrence, but it's really the same thing. It deters one and only one, in my opinion. Nobody ever made a successful survey that the death penalty ever deterred anyone else from killing or not killing someone and for me it's the ultimate punishment for an ultimate crime. With juries, however, bleeding hearts and those worried about the hereafter and their place in heaven, the death penalty doesn't get much traction with the 'life without parole' option given to juries."

"I like this guy," Finnegan said. "Who is he and I'll get him another beer on the house."

Spencer had hit all the right chords and was welcomed into the fraternal order of "I've Got Your Back", which he saw as a good start for the day and a good place to be.

"This is Spencer Tallbridge, our new assistant prosecutor, and I think he's going to fit in like that eight ball over there in the corner pocket," Salyers said, pointing to an easy pool shot about to be made by a player nearby.

On his way home to his apartment, Spencer considered his tally for the day. He had won a job in what could be considered to be the largest law firm in the county. He was on the right side of Arnold and had won Salyers as a probable friend. Amy was an excellent secretary, and even though his office had no windows, the lighting was good and the walls did not need painting. He had met the judge he would be working with who seemed competent and not overbearing. On the downside, he had his first run in with Molly McBride, which should have been expected because most all courthouses have a Molly McBride in one way or another, and he would just have to live with it, at least for a few more months. Still, he had a nagging feeling that always got him in trouble. "When something is too easy, it usually isn't," he thought. He felt the need to know more about Molly, welling up from his recent past as a defense attorney with a knack for asking too many questions and in spite of the warning from Arnold.

Chapter Four

Judge Harris was a kind soul, compassionate and soft spoken.

Spencer liked his approach. The first few cases were little more than motion hearings and Spencer's monitor, Salyers, was along to make sure Spencer did not miss anything important. What could not be missed was the expected verbal attack by Molly claiming that somehow and in some way Spencer was a murderer every time he approached the court room.

One morning, as he was walking the hall leading to the court room of Judge Harris, he saw Molly ahead as usual. She was by herself and no other persons waiting for court were in the hallway. Molly again made her singular claim and Spencer decided it was time to set her straight. Surely, he thought, he could overcome being sucked in like his unfortunate predecessor.

"Hello, Ms. McBride, do you know me?" he asked as Molly was about to make her usual announcement.

"I know you. I know all of you and you know me. And it's Mrs. McBride, if it's all the same to you."

"I understand. I meant no disrespect. It just seems that is how women are addressed these days. But I do want to know why you call me a murderer."

"I guess they didn't tell you or maybe you never asked, but you and everyone in your office is murdering my son and I won't let you forget it," she said clearly.

"Why me? I was just hired a month ago and we do not kill people," wondering where this was going next.

"It is you and all the rest of you because you are all I have left. You will take my son's life and he's all I have. He's a good boy – never hurt anyone – and you're going to kill him."

Spencer felt that at least he had her saying something new and maybe he could get to the bottom of her claim, if he could get her to say more.

"I really don't know what you are talking about and perhaps I should have asked you sooner or someone in my office. I really would like to know what you are talking about."

Spencer knew that Arnold was probably right. He could leave her alone and eventually she would leave or die or maybe he could just get her to leave him out of her apparent obsession with her son's case and that would be enough.

"I have a little time before court. Tell me, please, tell me what happened to your son."

"Well, you convicted him. You and your whole office are going to murder him."

"I have heard that for a month now and it does bother me. Really, I don't know what your problem is and your shouting murderer in public every time I walk by offends me."

"I hope so. Someone has to be offended. I'm offended. Everyone's offended. But nothing helps. It's just that he is all I have left. You're offended? What a joke," she scoffed. "You and your kind are killing my son, and this is all I have left."

Spencer was about to quit and move on. Perhaps it was time, he thought, to relegate Molly to the heap of poor deranged souls that no one can help or reason with. This was her life, to hear her tell it, and nothing Spencer could do would change it. But Spencer was curious. He was always curious. He always thought his curiosity was what made him a good lawyer, at least in his own mind. He was always compelled to ask one more question that could change his life for better or worse, if his curiosity took hold.

"Tell me," Spencer began with sympathetic sincerity, "how long has it been?"

"Twenty-six years, six months, twenty-two days and...." Molly looked up at the hallway clock, "...two hours and forty-seven minutes ago my son was convicted and sentenced to die by lethal injection for a crime he didn't commit. He is innocent and he will be gone."

Spencer suddenly realized he was embarking on ground that he should not be treading upon with her claim that her son was innocent. This was not his business even though it was his business. It was one of Herald's cases and one of his first death penalty cases. It was one he tried and was responsible for in his position as Prosecutor.

"Thank you, Mrs. McBride. I really didn't know any details and..."

Molly cut him off, "...and there is nothing you can do about it."

"I suppose so." Spencer hoped that concession would separate him from what she hated, but it was not to be.

"You are still a murderer," she again said with dismissive conviction. "Just go," looking down at her old, heavily worn shoes.

Spencer had no time for more and slowly stood up saying, "I do feel sorry for you, Mrs. McBride. I guess I can't expect the same from you, right?"

Without looking up she said sharply, "Right."

As Spencer entered the courtroom, all concerns for Molly disappeared. She was out of sight and out of mind, and he had the people's work to do. She would still be there on his return for another verbal declaration unless she found another assistant in another hallway to harass. For Spencer, she was not his problem, at least not one of his making. To him, she was just another lost soul and a mother with unconditional love for her son. Nothing new there. Spencer had seen this before many times as a defense attorney and there would be no convincing or reasoning with a parent claiming injustice of a child accused of a crime. Molly's son probably deserved what he will get, he thought, and even as a defense attorney Spencer never had a problem with the retribution part of the death penalty. For all its flaws and unequal application, case by case or state by state, Spencer always felt that there was something positive about an eye for an eye. For now, Spencer had arrived where the entire prosecutor's staff was regarding Molly and her place in the system of justice. As a former defense attorney, he was keenly aware that there are always victims on each of the most heinous crimes. Move on, case closed or so he thought.

Chapter Five

Spencer's secretary Amy Jacobs was better than advertised. She had been with the office for at least a decade and knew the ropes. She also kept it impersonal and stuck to the business at hand, but was not above getting to know more about Spencer than just his legal background. One morning when there was a pause in the hectic drive to move cases along, she saw that Spencer was relaxed and staring out his window. It presented an opportunity to get to know him.

"Well, Mr. Tallbridge, I mean Spencer, how do you like it so far?"

"It's all good," he responded. "I think the staff has been a great help, and you, of course. I was just thinking about how long this would all last. I mean, what I will be doing in ten years, fifteen years? You know, the assistants here are all dedicated and see themselves as career prosecutors..."

"Well, aren't they?" she interrupted.

"Yes, but it's just hard to imagine that we have all hit the end of the road as a career path."

"Perhaps if you were married," she injected, "and had a family to support, a 'career path' would not be as important to you."

How insightful, Spencer thought. She obviously heard others weigh the issue and came to the conclusion that being the way it is and will be is not so bad if there are other interests beyond the office.

"So, have you ever thought about marriage, a family? Ever had someone special?"

Spencer smiled and understood the depth of the question.

"Have I ever been in love you want to know? Well, yes. In college I was hopelessly in love with a storybook ending, but not for me. She ended up with a football hero and I eventually ended up with a law degree. They married and the hero became a baker; so I have always joked that she was finally rolling in dough."

"Sour dough!" she laughed loudly to make a pun invited by Spencer's story.

"No. Not really. I think he is a good man from what I have heard, but I try not to pay too much attention to old times and former girlfriends. I don't have much time for romance now and you know the policy here. I'm not planning to buy a minivan anytime soon."

"I know the policy, but you could be a good catch for someone outside the office. I mean you're an attorney and easy on the eyes, if you don't mind me telling you. I have friends that could be interested and interesting," she said inviting a positive reply.

"Thanks, but no thanks. At least for now."

"Maybe you need a dog," as Amy quickly changed the subject. "Where are you from? I can usually tell from an accent – New York, Boston, Harvard," she laughed, "but you seem to be Midwest."

"I am from out west, the cowboy states. As a kid we moved around a lot. My father is a farrier, so it was a country life."

"A furrier?" Amy asked "Doesn't seem to be much market for furs anymore. Did your dad trap or raise the furry little critters?"

Spencer paused a long time before answering. Amy didn't have a clue about what a farrier does, so he would have to educate her.

"It's not furs, it's horseshoes," he responded. "A farrier puts horseshoes on horses. It's a specialty in the horse trade and an important one."

"You mean he's a blacksmith then?" she asked.

"No, he gets the shoes from a blacksmith and he fits them to the hooves of a horse. He trims their hooves like fingernails to make them fit. Sort of like using that nail file I see you using from time to time. He uses a file, a big one called a rasp to make them fit."

"Is there any real money in that?" she asked.

"You would be amazed. A good farrier can make six figures with racehorses. Remember, those thoroughbreds can be worth millions so good shoes are important, and you can't entrust those feet to just anyone. Throw a shoe, lose a horse and that's a lot of money to risk on something that is supposed to bring good luck."

"Does your dad work with racehorses?"

"He did for a while when I was growing up and in college. It was easier to work with those, too. Racehorse shoes are made of aluminum and work horses use iron. That's where a blacksmith comes in. I think he liked the racehorses more than their owners, so he works around small farms with iron shoes now. He's sort of a snob in reverse," Spencer said with a laugh. "He's like a horse whisperer and has a lot of horse sense. I think he likes the farmer trade much more than the millionaires he used to work for. Probably accounts for why he went country and not big city after I got out of school."

"Where is he now? Do you see him often?"

"I don't see him much, but we talk on the phone. He works farms near Muskogee, Oklahoma. It's a little warmer there in the winter compared to where he worked in Cheyenne when I was a kid. He goes where the horses are like airplane mechanics and airplanes. My mother died in Cheyenne, too, when I was four so that might have something to do with his move to Muskogee." Amy started to sing "I'm just an Okey from Muskogee..."

"OK, OK, not really," he said disparagingly. "My roots are here now, but there is something to be said for the simplicity of 'home on the range' compared to what I do now, and no one calls me a murderer."

"You still haven't gotten past that crazy old lady's attacks, have you?" Amy asked. "You just need to keep her out of your head. I think you will eventually get used to her like everyone else. At least that is the way it seems to me. No one cares what she says anymore except, I guess, you. And besides after he's executed it will all be over. That's the way it goes around here. Here today, gone tomorrow," she said whimsically.

"I suppose you're right. It's just unsettling every time I walk by her, especially when people hear her and don't know what's going on. I can't stop and explain that she is just a nut and I have to put up with her. And there is nothing I can do about it." Spencer paused and recalled her same words "and there is nothing I can do about it".

There was a challenge and conflict in that. He felt the challenge without putting it to words and he believed also that Molly would never be over it regardless of the execution. Spencer grew up solving problems. Sitting at his father's knee, he watched as his father solved problems fitting horseshoes. No two were alike. Each one was a new problem. Each one had to be solved. He never looked at it that they were only horseshoes. He always knew that the horse could not do without them. It stood to reason that Spencer could solve the problem with Molly by explaining somehow that he and the office were not at fault. To solve it he decided he would have to learn more about what her problem was with the case against her son and it would not be long before another opportunity presented itself for that inquiry.

Chapter Six

Spencer rarely saw Arnold except at a distance, but he would stop by Spencer's office to test the waters with his usual question. "So, how's it going, kid?" and Spencer would respond, "Straight and level, Mr. Arnold. No bumps, no lumps, all's well so far."

On one such occasion Arnold added a note of praise to a murder case Spencer recently tried. "Nice work on the Phelps case. Not every day an assistant is lucky enough to get a Perry Mason moment."

Spencer thought about the "luck" word because his attack on Phelps on cross-examination was well planned with the desired result, but he let it pass. Arnold was referring to a trial that involved Phelps stabbing a fellow barfly, Big Red, to death at his trailer. Phelps claimed self-defense with mutual combat, and with dead men telling no tales, Spencer needed to show that Phelps was the aggressor and brought the knife into the fight that Phelps steadfastly denied to police. Spencer also knew that Phelps had to take the stand to make his case. Phelps could have relied on the transcript of his police interrogation, but Spencer was confident that the attorney for Phelps would not take that chance with a jury that would want to hear from his client on the witness stand.

Spencer had watched the interrogation of Phelps several times to understand the personality of the man he would have to challenge. Spencer knew that Phelps would be well prepared to stick to his story and that it would be the word of Phelps against no word from his victim. During the police interrogation, Spencer heard the detective tell Phelps he was a coward for using a knife, and Phelps reacted in anger. "I ain't no coward. I had to do it. He came at me with the knife. I just did what anybody would do. I ain't no coward," Phelps repeated throughout the questioning. He seemed unshakeable. It was such a close case Spencer wondered how it got out of the Grand Jury with an indictment, which happened before he was hired and, as the new guy, it was no surprise he would end up with the case. The surprise for everyone was the outcome.

As Spencer cross-examined Phelps, he purposely asked simple questions that gave Phelps an opportunity to relax on the stand and retell his story. As the questioning progressed, it seemed that Spencer was encouraging Phelps to gain even more confidence in his narration of events, and confidence that totally justified self-defense leaving the court room spectators to wonder if Spencer was throwing the case.

"So, the knife was absolutely brought to the fight by Big Red?"

"For sure; wasn't mine."

With that, Spencer took a long pause and looking at Phelps with a determined eye he cut into him with surgical precision, "Of course it was yours; you're a coward and got the knife from your mother."

Spencer's assertion about the mother of Phelps was less than a guess. He had no real thought that the knife came from his mother. He just knew that Phelps reacted to claims of cowardice and invoking his mother might just tip the reaction in Spencer's favor. The reaction of Phelps was knee-jerk rage, exactly as hoped for. Spencer had hit a nerve that he knew was exactly where he expected it to be and zeroed in on it with the accuracy of a sniper.

"That's bullshit. It was under my bed."

There was a sudden muffled groan across the courtroom and then silence that did not seem to end. The jurors looked around at each other in utter amazement with silent expressions of, "Did I just hear what I thought I heard?" Finally, Spencer broke into the stunned silence and said, "And that folks was the end of Big Red. No further questions." It was also the end for

Phelps, who was convicted in less than an hour of jury deliber-
ations and continues to stand for the trial lawyers' motto: "Lose
your cool, lose you case". For Spencer, the only downside was
knowing that Molly was outside as always and waiting to let him
know how she felt about his success. No victory lap there.

As months went by, Spencer began to rack up a record
that was competing with the other more seasoned trial attorneys
on staff. Spencer had a way of thinking on his feet that kept him
one step ahead of the competition on both sides. His Perry Mason
moment got him enough attention to place him in the rotation for
the most serious cases and especially the lost causes that every
prosecutor faces from time to time. With Spencer, his superiors
thought that lightning might be able to strike a second or even
a third time and, as the new guy, he knew from Salyers that the
Compton case would be his regardless of the probable outcome.
The Compton case was now five years old and the evidence was
as stale as week- old cold french fries. The assistant prosecutor
who was responsible for enough trial errors to secure the rever-
sal had moved on to a defense practice and no one wanted to be
in the rotation for the retrial. Salyers initially thought it would
fall on him since the case was assigned to Judge Harris where he
prosecuted. But eventually Arnold gave Spencer the assignment
as now expected.

"You will have a lot to reconstruct," Arnold said, when he
gave Spencer the case. "I will have Central Records pull the file
and evidence. I would have one of the investigators start locating
the witnesses once you get this organized, but that's up to you. I
hope you're not pissed at getting this one."

"How long will it take to get the file?" Spencer asked without comment on the pissed issue.

"Probably next week. They are always short staffed over
there, but I will see what I can do to speed things up. Good luck,
kid," Arnold said, using his standard line as he moved on.

Spencer had also heard about the case from others who
were on staff during the trial. It was defended on the basis that
the defendant, John Michael Compton, was in a love triangle
with the victim and her daughter and that it was the daughter
who assaulted her mother. There was no alibi for Compton other
than his claim that he was never at the crime scene in a city park.

The head of the victim had been bludgeoned and a wooden stake was found nearby with hair fibers imbedded in the tip. Those were examined and found to be consistent with the victim's hair, but no other tests were performed. It immediately struck Spencer that more needed to be done than just a repeat performance by a new assistant prosecutor. The following week the case file came in with a one volume transcript and a list of evidence. The stake was listed and Spencer called for an investigator to retrieve it.

"I need you to find a piece of evidence in the Compton case from Central Records. When you find it, do not open its package. Just please bring it to me. According to the trial transcript, it's a wooden stake about two feet long and six inches wide. The package will have the case name and number so it should be easy to find."

The investigator looked at him quizzically as if to say, "Really?"

The next day the investigator reported regretfully that the stake was nowhere to be found. He searched every box of evidence and every nearby box of unrelated evidence with the records clerk in an attempt to locate it with no success. This experience was a first for Spencer but was not a first for the prosecutor's office. Keeping track of evidence requires dedication and putting people in charge of evidence who have no concept of how important accuracy can be results in occasional problems that can have devastating results.

"Well, I guess I will take a look and see what I can find. I need to see how Central Records works anyway," as Spencer thanked the investigator for his effort. It was at this time that Spencer began to seriously consider a plan to look at the case against Molly's son. Because he would be going into Central Records on a search anyway, he figured that no harm could be done by taking a look at the McBride case at the same time. But then again, maybe there might be. What if, he thought, Prosecutor Herald found out he was snooping around in one of his death penalty cases on appeal without telling him? What then? What seemed like a good and easy solution suddenly started to look deceptive and a problem.

That night Spencer called his father. It was not out of the ordinary. He often called his father to make sure he was all right and hadn't been kicked in the head by a horse. But on the McBride case there wasn't anyone on staff that he could trust to talk about looking into it in spite of his good intentions. He considered Salyers, but quickly dismissed him as one with mixed loyalties and probably limited ones for Spencer this early in his tenure. Especially if, as he suspected, Salyers was tasked with keeping an eye on him.

"Hello, Dad. How's it going?"

"Good to hear from you, son. How's the family crime fighter?"

"Well enough," which was not his usual answer to the usual question.

"OK, so what's on your mind, son?" he asked understandingly.

Spencer immediately knew that small talk was out, and he could get to the point of what was bothering him about the McBride case.

"It could be a long story, but the short story is that I'm concerned that I am about to do something stupid that could cost me my job."

"No harm, no foul so far, right?" his father asked with guarded anticipation that Spencer was not yet in trouble.

"No foul yet, but I'm trying to help someone understand the good we do here, and the only way I see doing that is to stick my nose where it doesn't belong and that might result in it getting cut off. I have to look at an old file, but looking at it may get me in trouble with my boss. It's a serious case, a death penalty case, and an execution will take place shortly this year. There is no stopping that, but at this point my looking at the file may draw unwanted attention and right now I don't need that. I just feel that by getting into this I am doing something dishonest. Well, not dishonest, but against my conscience."

"You mean against your better judgment? Why do you have to be the one in the first place with this undertaking? What is it to you? Why the hell you?" he said with more force in his voice with each question.

"That's the longer story. There is a mother of the guy who is going to be executed. She sits outside the courtrooms and calls all the assistant prosecutors murderers. It is wearing me down and I feel sorry for her. She has no understanding of the legal system, just a blind mother's love for her criminal son and frankly her son – a murdering rapist –deserves to die. I just can't get past the idea that I am breaching loyalty to my boss, if I start poking around and..."

"And I am supposed to give you absolution in advance? Son, I just fit horseshoes, but I have always told you that things fit when they are done right, and you will always know when something does not fit. Wishing that those fit never works. Sometimes you have to work around a problem and not hit it head on. Seems to me you ought to be able to think of a way to make things fit, but I'm no lawyer. I'll leave that to you. Knowing you, it seems you are trying hard to convince yourself about just how guilty this guy really is to keep out of what you do best, asking questions."

What Spencer heard was not what he expected. He half expected his father to say "stop with the bleeding heart stuff". Instead he was suggesting without saying more that Spencer solve the problem. Somehow, he had to make it fit.

"Well, son," he continued, "this all seems to remind me of a problem I had with old Bill Burnside. I could never convince him of anything, but if I was able to figure out a way to make it his idea, I got it done. Saved a few of his horses and sounds like you might consider that."

Spencer saw immediately what he meant and felt embarrassed that he did not think of the solution himself. Maybe, he thought, he was just too close to the problem, but it was another lesson learned.

"Don't forget what I have always told you. We are both in sales. I sell shoes. You sell what you do. Justice I hope, but it's all sales and I think you have done a damn good job so far and I am proud of you. But whatever you are selling just be careful. Don't grind into the quick."

Spencer had heard that expression "don't grind into the quick" many times over the years from his dad. There was a life lesson there. Grind too far with anything and all hell could break loose. With a wounded horse or a business deal gone sour, bad things will always happen if you grind into the quick.

"Got it, Dad. I will stay out of the quick. And thanks. I needed that."

Chapter Seven

Spencer called ahead to make an appointment to speak with Prosecutor Herald. There was a loose chain of command so he could not just drop in. Although he had not cleared the meeting with Arnold, Herald told him to stop by that morning. It was the first time he had been to meet with Herald since he was hired, and he did not feel the same pressure as before, but pressure nonetheless from knowing that he was not going to be entirely forthright with his boss.

"Good to see you, Tallbridge. I suppose you're here to complete your victory lap following your big win. Not many people around here remember Perry Mason, but it seems you've had a little of his success."

"Not really. Some might also think it was just plumb dumb luck and it might have been."

"I wanted to see you to congratulate you. So, what's on your mind?" Herald said.

"I'm looking for some advice. You are the champ around here on murder cases and I have a tough felonious assault case coming up. I suppose I could get some tips from the team, but I thought I would just come to the source and see if you have any old closed cases I could review to get a handle on preparation – investigation reviews – stuff like that. I'm not looking for a seminar from you and I expect you think I already know my job, but I have always wondered how you did it so successfully all these years."

Spencer put the bait in the water and now he just had to hope and wait for a bite. It didn't take long.

"Well, Spencer, I'm flattered you hold me in such high regard. I like war stories and I really like to tell them. The problem with war stories is they take too long and right now I just don't have that much time. If you are really that interested in what I have done, go down to Central Records and get a few of the trial transcripts on my cases. They are all there. Just about every case was appealed and never successfully, so whatever I did in those should still stand up. Don't get too bogged down by the law in those days. Things have changed. If you need to, get a list from Arnold. He was around most of that time and followed me close. He might be of some help. I appreciate your desire to learn more than by just being kicked around the court room. When I was your age that is how I learned and I still have the scars to prove it," he said with a laugh.

"Yes, sir. I'm not sucking up. I just figure I could save some time by listening to the master and reviewing – I mean studying – your work, does seem like the fast track. Thank you."

That meeting was a big relief for Spencer. Plan, bait and execution worked like a charm. The pressure was off. He could look at the McBride case and not feel the slightest bit of guilt that somehow he was working against his boss, his office, and the oath of office he took the first day he was hired. Now he wouldn't have to ask Arnold for a list. Now all he had to do was find the time to work both cases together. One was the Compton assault case pending and the other the McBride case that he needed to understand to convince Molly that at least he was not a murderer. The best place to start, he thought, was to pay Molly a visit.

Chapter Eight

Molly was easy to find. One simple question to one of the office investigators about her address and the first one asked had it without looking it up. They all knew who she was through the years and had some concerns about her mental stability and potential for violence. She lived near the courthouse in a downtown apartment off the main street through town. Molly was poor and had nothing except her sorrow and hatred that kept her going. For her, that was enough.

It was early on a Tuesday evening when Spencer knocked on her door.

"Who is it?" she responded through the door.

"It's Spencer Tallbridge, from the courthouse. We talked a week or so ago, and I would like to talk to you."

"I know you want me to stop like all the rest. I won't. Just go. Leave me alone," Molly demanded.

"I really just want to help." Spencer knew that was only a half truth and the only way to convince Molly to open her door. He wanted to help himself, and to do so he would have to convince Molly that her son got a fair trial and the outcome was just. He did not consider that Molly would never accept anything except vindication. To Spencer the record of truth and justice should prevail, and she would have a better life if only the truth was shown to her.

Cautiously, Molly opened the door, moved no doubt by the offer of help. As Spencer expected that was too much for her to resist. It was a long time since she had heard those words.

"How can you help now? It's too late." She began to tear up, but opened the door further signaling that Spencer could come in and continue with whatever he had to say.

Molly's apartment was dimly lit, and the smell of stale tobacco hung in the air. It was a small, two-room, no frills, third-floor apartment with no elevator. There were a few books and mostly old magazines piled randomly on a small table with an ash tray filled to near capacity sitting prominently on top. Next to it was the only comfortable looking chair in the room and it was covered in a tattered plaid blanket hiding the well-worn fabric underneath. This was not a room where quests were expected and not a room where appearances meant anything to Molly.

"Molly, I don't mind telling you I am deeply troubled by your statement to me that your son is innocent. I am not here to convince you otherwise."

Molly broke in, "You probably think I am stupid and can't accept the truth. I know he was convicted and his appeal said he must…" Molly choked. She could not get the word out.

"So how can I be right," she continued, "and everyone else in the world is wrong? Everyone who is smarter and richer than me says that I am just a fool, just some kind of nut. Let me tell you, I know my son and he is no murderer. You and your kind are the murderers here."

Suddenly Spencer felt like he was back in the court hallway with Molly once again on the attack. Now fortunately he had more time beyond just fending off the arrows shot at him.

"Tell me. Please tell me. Why is it more than just your love for your son that tells you he is innocent? Do you mind if I sit down for a minute just to talk?" Spencer asked as he reached for a small wooden kitchen-type chair.

"OK. Careful. It's kind of rickety. Hasn't anyone told you? Hasn't anyone told you my son was with me the whole time he was supposedly raping and murdering that girl? No one believed him when he told the police the first time and no one believed me either," Molly said, as she sat back into the plaid covered chair and lit a cigarette.

"Molly, I haven't read the case yet, but I was told briefly that it was open and shut as the police say. Your son confessed," Spencer said with assertive emphasis.

"He eventually said he did it, but it was no confession. A confession states truth. A false statement is no confession. Do you get it?"

It seemed to Spencer that a switch was thrown, and she no longer sounded like a crazy woman, but was talking like a schooled attorney, probably from years of association with her sense of the facts of the case, and he was now being cross examined. He did not answer. Spencer had seen many cases with claims that someone was in two places at the same time and couldn't be in two places at the same time. Somehow Molly had to be wrong, and the trial transcript would solve her problem with her memory which is where the problem usually was. It never occurred to him that she was simply lying. Her sincerity was overpowering to eliminate that. She now held firmly to her belief and changing that seemed impossible regardless of her son's guilt. Spencer decided to change the subject to something kinder and friendlier.

"Tell me about your son. I know it has been hard on you after all this started, but I would like to know more about him."

"Why? What good will it do. You want me to like you, so I won't hate you. I know what you're doing. You don't like my Billy."

"No. Honestly, I don't like what he did and…"
Molly's expression turned sour and she started to get up from her chair.

"Look," Spencer injected, "I'm just a lawyer going from the record. I wouldn't be here if I didn't think something needs to be straightened out."

He left out telling Molly he planned to convince her with a proof beyond a reasonable doubt that her son was a murderer and not his innocence. If somehow she would face the truth, her life and his would no doubt be better, or so he thought.

Molly settled back into her chair again and began. Still suspect of Spencer's motives, she told the story of her son coloring it like something out of a Norman Rockwell painting.

"Billy was always a good boy. Other kids would get in trouble, but not Billy. He was born on March 11, 1962. His father was with me when he was born. Our only child. A boy for his father and a good boy. My Tony worked hard to provide a good home for us. We didn't have a lot, but we had the parks in the summer and Billy did well in school. He always wanted to help others. Carry someone's groceries. Shovel someone's snow for free. Rake someone's leaves for free. He would have mowed grass for free, if he had the money for gas which he didn't. Everyone thought how terrible it was that such a good boy could commit such horrible crimes. The same people that thought so well of him were just as quick to condemn him. They all thought since Tony died in a car accident that Billy went bad from not having a father and all. Billy did take losing his father hard. Tony was everything to him. Sure, it hurt. We hurt together, but he didn't go bad because of that. He didn't go bad, period."

"Did Billy know the woman who was murdered?"

"Yes. He knew her. Like everyone, she took a liking to him he told me later. She asked him to help her fix some things around her apartment, and people saw him going there a few times and that's how the police came up with him as the one who did it."

"The classic no good deed going unpunished, right?" Spencer asked.

"You could say that."

"Did you testify?" Spencer asked.

"Of course. It didn't go well. Herald confused me on the date. I know I had it right, but it came out wrong. I don't know how that happened. I guess I just looked like a mother trying to save her son and I ended up helping to convict him," as her voice seemed to choke again on the words.

"It's not your fault," Spencer volunteered. "Without an impartial witness to support your son, it was probably hopeless from the beginning unless the police were lying."

"They were. They had to be. I know the truth. My son was with me."

From his experience now on both sides, Spencer knew she probably got the dates mixed up. The date and time of events are always hard to confirm unless there is independent hard evidence and a mother's claim alone carries little weight. Spencer thought it was a good time to change the subject.

"I see you have books about dogs?" They were scattered on the few tables in her room. "Do you have a dog?" Spencer asked to talk about something that might be pleasant but forgetting the impossibility of having a dog in a third-floor apartment.

"I have no dog. I only get Social Security which is just enough to get by. We had a dog once. It was Billy's and he loved it, but Sport, that was the name Billy gave it, got sick – real sick – and had to be put to sleep. I would like another dog. It would be something to care for, but I can't bring myself to care for anything. Can you understand that?"

"I do. I feel the emptiness here and I don't think I can change that. Has anyone ever tried to help?"

"You mean more lawyers?"

"Yes"

"He has lawyers. Lots of lawyers. They all think he is guilty. Their only interest is stopping the death penalty. They hate it more than they want to help Billy. They really do not care about Billy. They have asked me to write letters and I write letters. Whatever they want, I do. It's just not enough and now it's almost over for Billy, but it will never end for me until I'm dead, too. After he's gone, they will be gone. The lawyers, I will never see or hear from them again. I know it. It will just be over for them. Next case and the same for you."

"But if he did do…"

Molly broke in, "He didn't. He didn't do it. I am not mistaken now. Herald got me to make a mistake then, but I am not mistaken. He didn't do it," she shouted.

"Do you see Billy very often?" It was an awkward question in the hope of calming Molly down. He anticipated the answer. Molly could barely survive on what she had and left nothing for travel.

"No. I write letters. That's all I can do. Billy says he does not want to see me because it hurts too much. He wants me to forget him. He thinks that will make it easier on me. He said they will just put him to sleep like Sport and that will be it. I did visit for a for a few years when I could save up enough for the bus ride, but the visits hurt too much for both of us, so I stopped. Have you ever been to a prison? Do you have any idea what it's like?"

"Not that prison, no. But I have been to prisons and jails, so I think I understand."

"I doubt it. It is horrible. You feel it all the way there, all the time you're there, and all the way back. And there will come a time when it will be…" she stopped short again holding back the word that would spell the end.

"What about phone calls? Can he call you?"

Spencer knew from his experience with general felony cases that calls were permitted but was unaware that no calls were permitted while awaiting execution.

"No, and he wouldn't even if he could. He wants me out of his life. I think it helps him cope with what's coming. It's called death row. That's not some made up word. That is the title of the place he is at and the rule is 'no calls. Not that it would make any difference, but I know his voice. I hear it at night. I hear him calling. Calling me…" as her voice trailed off to somewhere else.

Spencer decided he had spent enough time to understand the world and reality where Molly lived. There was probably not much he could do except to assuage his own curiosity and just maybe help Molly understand that Billy's fate was not her fault. He left without leaving Molly any hope. There wasn't any to leave. He saw none and expected even less. For Spencer, hope would be a new burden, and he had second thoughts about his anticipated involvement. He would just take it one day at a time like every case he ever handled and his hope for himself was to just see it through to the end with a good fit like a horseshoe. As he considered his next day, he played over in his mind his father's admonition: "Just don't grind into the quick."

Chapter Nine

The next day Spencer had time scheduled to visit Central Records to look for the exhibit in the Compton case and ask for a copy of the McBride transcript of trial proceedings. It was the records depository for the records of all county office holders and was one of those WPA projects repurposed for records storage where the lights are never fully working and the records are kept in lightless metal cabinets where the dust dances in the light when anything or anybody moves by them. It was an imposing structure. Built in the mid-1930s, it was more like an antique than anything functional. There were four floors and three employees who worked like librarians to keep everything catalogued and safe.

"Hello. I am Spencer Tallbridge and I am here to review a few cases," Spencer said to a clerk he met seated at a desk at the entrance.

"Nice to meet you; Who are you with? I mean, do you work for the county? Or…"

"I'm an assistant prosecutor. Have been for about four months and never made it over here. Usually my office just sends out for copies of files, but there are some things that you may not be able to send or find so I just thought I would drop in and take a look."

"Sure. I will need to see your I.D. and please sign in. Nothing goes out unless we say so, but if you need a copy of anything, just let me know. No charge for county offices. You will use one of the file review rooms," she instructed.

Spencer had a badge by this time and proudly showed it to her. It was the first time he used it officially, although it did come in handy with a traffic stop for speeding. Maybe he simply got off with just a warning or maybe there really was something to professional courtesy. After signing in, he got started.

"So how can I help you?" the clerk asked politely.

"Well, it's an old case, but has come up for a retrial. I have a copy of the transcript and a list of all the exhibits. I need to see the exhibits and one in particular. I was told that it's missing, and I want to see for myself."

"We don't lose exhibits," the clerk noted disdainfully.

"I'm sure you don't. How long have you been here doing this job?"

"I retire next year with my thirty and the others have been here almost as long. We know our job and I think we do it well for such an understaffed office. Not that anyone cares," she said with a laugh.

"I am sure you do. I didn't mean to imply you don't. I expect there is a lot of skill keeping everything straight. Probably a lot of stuff comes in every day."

"You might say we are underappreciated until something is lost and can't be found. Then we get appreciated until we find it. We're trying to go over to all digital files, but that takes time and then there are still the exhibits."

"I fully understand and, as I said, that is why I am here. I sent an investigator over to locate an exhibit that will have to be checked out – I mean signed out – probably both – and so far, it seems to be lost. I am hoping you can help."

"Fill out this request form," the clerk instructed, "and we will have another look. I seem to remember someone from your office here last week and the problem you are talking about. I can have another look."

"Would it be OK, if I came along?" Spencer asked.

"I am not supposed to but, being from your office, I can make an exception. If you can't trust a prosecutor, who can you trust? Just don't mention it, OK? The two other women I work with leave in ten minutes. We will have a look after that."

"Secret's safe with me," he remarked.

Spencer was impressed with the apparent good impression he had made. Was it him or just his badge that made such a difference that she was willing to break a rule? He couldn't tell, but the opportunity to make a friend here might prove invaluable and he intended to take full advantage of the opportunity to do some friendly ingratiating.

"Thank you and I do appreciate you and your work. What is your name?"

"Laura Renner," the clerk said.

A few minutes near the closing hour, the other two records clerks began to orbit near the exit. Laura explained to them that she was helping a new assistant prosecutor locate a file and would close up shortly. After they left, the search began in earnest. Together they made their way to the second floor which was dedicated to criminal cases. There were dozens of large metal racks, six-feet tall, fully motorized to rotate them, and each had identification numbers corresponding to the case files they held. It may not have been the Dewey Decimal library system, but it served the purpose of linear location by case numbers and dates. Opposite the racks were cabinets equally as tall and under lock and key that held exhibits that were identified in each case. Apparently, this is where the search for the missing board started and recently concluded.

"So, what exactly are you looking for?"

"It's not a paper document. It's an exhibit. It's a wooden board that may have been used to assault a woman and I will need it for the retrial."

Laura's work with old and dusty records did not require her to dress in business attire. Pants with pockets were the standard for her and a short smock that kept dirty files from soiling her blouse. Laura reached into her pocket and came up with a set of keys on a short stick and quickly found the one that worked the exhibit locker where the board was supposed to be.

"Doubt they just missed it, but let's take a look."

It only took a moment to see that there was nothing that even remotely looked like the size of the described board or an evidence package of the same dimension.

"Sorry, not here. Just to be sure I want to open every locker in this series because it may be misfiled. Wouldn't be the first time, but I think that has already been done."

Spencer stood by as Laura again got out her keys and went to work. After a diligent search, she again turned up nothing. As she was looking, Spencer saw that there were what appeared to be exhibits lying on top of the cabinets.

"What's the stuff that looks like exhibits on top of the cabinets?" Spencer asked.

"As you probably can see, those are exhibits that are too big for the inside, so we just put them on top. I know it's not very secure, but until we get bigger cabinets, it's the best we can do. We never have had a security problem, but I think we run a pretty tight ship."

As Spencer acknowledged agreement, he asked "Is it possible that the exhibit fell behind the cabinet, if someone put it on top. I mean it's just a board – not a firearm."

"Possible, but we can't look from the end with this cabinet in the middle of all of these and we can't pull the cabinet out."

Spencer considered the one and only unspoken approach and he knew he would have to be the one to climb on top of the cabinet and look down with a flashlight which his cell phone would provide.

"Looks like I am elected to look from top down. Is there a step ladder around here?"

"Yes. It's where we entered this floor. I'll get it, but I think you are wasting your time. Nothing was ever lost like that. This might be a first."

As Laura walked away, Spencer noticed that the locks were all old-style door key type locks and not the barrel type found on vending machines. Spencer considered that record storage had obviously not kept up with more modern times. Laura returned with a step ladder and a hand full of rags.

"If you are going up there you are going to need these. I doubt that the tops of these have ever been cleaned."

"You mean if you don't bother it, it won't bother you," he remarked with a laugh.

"Exactly."

Spencer climbed his way up and cleaned a path through the dust on the cabinet top where the board may have been. He knew that no success would mean more cabinets and more cleaning, so he hoped for success on the first try. He slid across the top as he cleaned and when he got to the back, he pulled out his phone, hit the flashlight prompt, and looked down behind the cabinet. By then his only thought was, "Don't drop the phone." "It's there. It's got to be it. I see it. It's wrapped up, but it has to be it. Now all we have to do is find a way to get it." Spencer was almost euphoric. It was a break he had not expected.

"Congratulations, but not tonight," Laura said. "It hasn't gone anywhere for years and another day won't make a difference. I'll have maintenance get it for you tomorrow, if that works for you."

"Not really, unless you want to get a trial subpoena as a witness along with the guy from maintenance," Spencer said. "I need to be here for chain of custody issues and to prove that the lost board was really lost and really found," he said with a laugh.

"I understand and no, I don't want to go to court. See you in the morning. Thanks for finding it – I think," as she put her ring of cabinet keys in her pocket and escorted Spencer to the lobby.

"One last thing," Spencer added, "I would like a copy of the trial transcript in the William McBride murder case and its case number..."

Laura interrupted, "Know it by heart. I have been asked for stuff from that file for years and I should have a copy of the transcript for you tomorrow from the extra ones in the file by the time you get here. Are you working on this case? I thought it was over. I heard the time was up and a final execution date is set."

"No, I'm not working on it. I just want to see how Herald works and the best place to start is where he started years ago."

"You will read about my brother," Laura said. "He was a detective on that case and another one sort of like it after that too, but I don't think he was too involved. He's retired and I think he's glad to be away from all that stuff."

"I'm sure he is. If you see him tell him I said hello," seeking to add to his new friendship with the clerk and apparent confidant with her slightly bent procedures. "See you tomorrow."

Chapter Ten

Spencer arrived at his apartment and felt relieved that he had made some progress on the Compton assault case scheduled for retrial and was on his way to an understanding of the McBride case. After fixing one of his best recipes, five minutes on high and stir, he settled back to plan his next day after locating what he hoped to be the long-lost evidence and the McBride trial transcript. It was time for a break. Spencer played the guitar poorly, but felt that he relaxed best when he played the worst. It was something fun that he would never share. It was a solitary activity and making up a song or two let him leave the world of crime and punishment for a daydream of stardom as a musician that would never happen. He titled a song that he was working on "Those Five to Ten Blues". It told the story of a good-hearted bank robber with very bad luck and an equally unsympathetic judge. Spencer began to sing:

"Five to ten, five to ten," he said, "Oh, no!" And the judge said it again.

"Five to ten, you need to go, and I'll be glad when you're in the pen."

He said, "Five to ten will wear out my shoes.

You're giving me those Five to Ten Blues."

As bad as the song was, Spencer enjoyed putting the words and simple chords together, but this song struck a discord knowing that McBride was facing death, and nothing would change that. The blues did not fit. His simple goal was, and had to be, convincing Molly that she was not at fault for her son's conviction and upcoming execution. Nothing she could have said would have changed that result and he was sure the transcript would be the solution.

The next morning, Spencer arrived at Central Records, and Laura Renner was also there with a maintenance employee.

"How do you propose to fish out the board?" Spencer asked the fellow from maintenance.

"I plan on doing just that. I have this pole with a loop and rope. I just have to slip the rope over and pull it out."

"Works for me. Let's do it."

The three went to the second floor and the procedure began. Carefully, the maintenance man lowered the pole and loop behind the cabinet, raised it, and out came the board delivered into Spencer's waiting hands. The board was packaged in a sealed evidence wrapper with markings from the Compton case. It did not appear to have ever been opened and would remain sealed until it could be opened in the presence of the defense attorney. Only then could he submit it for further tests that had not been performed the first time around, and Spencer had been given a free hand to conduct any tests he deemed necessary.

"I guess I need to sign this out?" Spencer asked Renner.

"Just sign here and I also have the McBride transcript for you. It's in six binders. Do you want to take them now or do you want me to send them over?"

"I just need the trial manuscript. I don't need the court of appeals stuff but would like any motions that came after the trial dealing with evidence."

"I think I have included what you want – Herald's trial work – and what happened a few years back regarding DNA testing," Renner said.

"That should do it and if you have a cart, I will just take it with me."

Spencer did not want to be looking over the McBride case in his office and felt it would be best if he simply took it home where he could review it at his leisure with plenty of spare time and no questions asked. He saw no need to remind anyone, especially Herald, that he was taking a second critical look at Herald's work that would lead to the eventual execution of Molly's son.

When Spencer got back to his office, he called Arnold to let him know that he found what he hoped with any luck and modern technology would be decisive evidence in the retrial of the Compton case.

"So, what's your plan?" Arnold said. "We have never had a case with evidence lost over such a long time. Not sure if you can make anything out of it, but I suppose it's worth a try."

"I need to let the defense know ASAP and get them over here to take a look at it. After that my plan is to get in touch with the state lab and see what they might be able to do with it."

"Just make sure no one touches it. Not even you without gloves. I had a case once where the defense as well as their client wanted to handle an exhibit to contaminate it before it was tested. Fortunately, thinking the worst of them, I was able to avoid that."

"Don't worry about that happening. It seems to be standard practice by some attorneys, I mean defense attorneys, to get away with that and I'm on to it. I keep a box of rubber gloves in my briefcase just in case."

Spencer made a call to the lead defense attorney, Marshall Fox, and told him about the new/old evidence. Fox was a solid defense attorney with skills. His talent was in his ability to string evidence together to tell the story he wanted told and not the one promoted by the prosecution. He was able to combine sincerity with emphasis to convince a jury that he, at least, believed in his case. Spencer also knew that he and Marshal were in the early phase of a courtroom dance and that all appearances between them were probably deceptive to throw the other off balance. Fox probably wasn't being paid well, but that would not detract from his dedication to win his case. For Spencer, the board might be the linchpin to the prosecution and Spencer wanted to move the case along to the scientific examination as quickly as possible. Marshall Fox did not waste any time in coming to Spencer's office to examine the board.

"Good to see you, Marshall, and thanks for coming over."

"No problem. I doubt the board has any value after all this time, but I understand your interest," Fox opined hoping to mute Spencer's interest in it.

Spencer had thoroughly read the trial transcript and was fully aware of the alibi defense. The defendant was locked into it at trial and nothing would change that. Spencer had not seen the board; it was still wrapped in evidence packaging. He was also aware that it had never been tested because it was rough wood that contained no visible signs, such as blood, indicating use as a weapon except a few strands of hair at the end that were visually consistent with the hair of the victim. At the time of the trial, DNA was not in widespread use. It was known, but not fully understood and labs had limited training in the science. Labs in those early days did everything possible to say no to such an examination because of the time involved and the DNA of the defendant had not even been taken. Most importantly, the board was apparently a detective's afterthought at the crime scene, and no one else ever gave it any weight from its appearance, in spite of the hair strands which were not conclusive of anything.

"I intend to look for possible contact DNA and fortunately it was obtained when Compton was sentenced after his conviction, so I won't have to bother you with a motion for it."

"That's a long shot, Spencer. What makes you think there is going to be anything found? You know I have to object to its use. Who knows where this board has been all this time with possible contamination."

"I know, but think it through. There might be contamination say from a hundred people, but there is nothing that says your client ever touched this before, during or after the last trial and the evidence wrapper is totally intact. With your client saying he was never at the scene, if his DNA is on the board, I see it as game over. That's why I asked you here. You and I will open this together with gloves on and you can try to make something out of this process as best you can."

"Well, aren't you?" Marshal questioned.

"Sure, but I don't make the facts and I hold the opinion that you, as his attorney, know more about the facts than I do so I am just trying to catch up."

Spencer and Marshall stretched on blue nitrile gloves – standard in work with evidence in criminal cases – and Spencer took several photographs of the evidence package from various perspectives before opening it. Once accomplished, Spencer took out his pocketknife that he always kept handy for just such purposes and carefully cut the end paper to remove the board. Following this he again photographed it and asked Marshall if he wanted to handle it or take his own photographs.

"No need. With my luck I'll breathe on it and leave my own DNA to become a mystery man in this case until you can show it's mine," Marshall said with a laugh.

"Interesting problem. I want to avoid that too," Spencer added while remembering the DNA discussion he had with Herald on his first day.

After the formalities were concluded, Spence repackaged the exhibit in Marshall's presence and set it aside. They talked small talk for a while. Spencer expected Marshall to probe about expectations on a verdict and Spencer did not go there. He had been there before as a defense attorney and knew that nothing would ever be asked or stated for sheer academic interest. It was like the bow before the dance began, and neither wanted to give the other any sense of an edge or who was leading the dance.

"Well, I guess that's all folks," Marshall said like a Bugs Bunny cartoon character. "Let me know when you find something out on your big idea. Find out how long it's going to take with the trial coming up in a couple of months and I may want to challenge anything that works against the defendant. You know without anything new, I just see a repeat performance for both of us," he said as he left Spencer's office.

He was probing after all, Spencer thought. Marshall hoped it would be a repeat trial with Spencer limited to the evidence at the first trial. Perhaps Marshall could come up with a few new wrinkles to take Spencer by surprise. Perhaps Marshall could put him to sleep with a repeat of old evidence and then wake him up when it was too late as a door slammed shut. Such is the way defense attorneys think. No truth, just strategy. That was always the downside of defense work. It was usually just a high stakes game. Like an old timer in the defense trade once said, "If all else fails, go with the truth."

Chapter Eleven

Spencer put in a call to the state laboratory to talk with Rob Patterson, the chief DNA analyst. Spencer hadn't yet had any contact with Patterson since taking his new position, and it was likely that Patterson did not know that Spencer was now an assistant prosecutor with a prosecution case on his hands. Fortunately, Spencer had not burned any bridges with Patterson as a defense attorney and to Spencer, Patterson was just a lab rat who knew his business. He was slightly older than Spencer and appeared to be a younger version of Arnold with thinning hair, glasses and the straight forward demeanor of an accountant. Spencer was fully aware of his credentials. He was "magna cum" everything in the world of chemistry. As a graduate of eastern Ivy League schools, he wondered why Patterson wasn't in a more lucrative business than solving criminal cases. Of course, it was always possible that he just liked the challenge with the people involved instead of just a rack of test tubes in the commercial world. More likely, he was simply a scientist without a business sense or motivation to make money. In government, he had the security to ultimately be himself in his own world governed by the periodic table of elements and not people.

"Hello, Mr. Patterson. This is Spencer Tallbridge and I will be working with you shortly. Remember me?" Spencer asked hopefully.

"Hi, Spencer. Yes, I do remember you and I'm not sure where this is going – you being on the other side. Do I have a case with you?"

"Yes, and not yet," Spencer responded. "I'm now an assistant prosecutor for Rutledge County and I have a case, but you have not been involved. I want to change that. I have a piece of evidence that was picked up at a crime scene and it could make a big difference with an alibi defense if the defendant's DNA is on it."

"So, what is it?"

"It's a board. Like a piece of old gray barn wood about three feet long, six inches wide and an inch thick. There is no obvious material on it except hair fibers in the tip consistent with hair from the victim from earlier tests. Sort of like the one case you testified about a few years ago."

"I do remember. Seems to me you got quite a lesson in that case and you were decent about it. Sorry."

"No apology needed. I did need a lesson and could use a few more instead of the ass kicking you gave me with that first lesson. My thinking is that the detective, who died last year, picked up the board with something in mind because of the hair fibers. From what I can tell from the transcript, the board never made it into the collection of stuff taken at the crime scene and was never scientifically examined beyond the fiber comparison that did not include the defendant. The prosecutors on the case thought it was a slam dunk without scientific evidence, but it's back for a retrial and a lot of the slam dunk stuff has been kicked out on the appeal. So here I am and the only piece of hard evidence I have is this board that may mean something or nothing. And that's where you come in."

"I would have thought it would have been examined the first time around with everything else when we first got the case. Do you have a record of what was sent up here?"

"I do and it's not on the list. Interestingly, it still made it to the case file in Central Records, and I actually found it behind a cabinet where, until I opened it today with the defense attorney, it has been for years in its original unopened evidence package."

"Hope you didn't mess it up. I mean I hope you didn't touch it with your hands."

"We did, but with gloves. I did learn. Remember?"

"I do. Glad to hear you are finally putting my lessons to good use! You mentioned the detective who found it is dead so if he needs to be excluded or identified, I will need DNA from a family member."

"That probably won't be necessary unless I inadvertently open Pandora's Box with DNA from an unknown. Anyone could have touched it, I suppose, but I am gambling that if any DNA is found it will be from the defendant who claims he wasn't there. I'll cross the unknown DNA bridge, if I get to it. The defense never asked to have it tested and is leaving it to me. In fact, the defense never mentioned it in the first trial, which tells me there is something there they already know. And if they are convinced his DNA is not on it, if they really think he's innocent, I expect they would be demanding an exam. For me it's a calculated risk."

"OK, just as long as you know what you are getting into and have thought it through. I always thought you guys never ask a question you don't know the answer to."

"Ordinarily you're right, but to every rule there is an exception, and this is one for me to make. I'll take my chances," Spencer explained.

"Well, make sure I get all the identification of the defendant in the first trial so I can look up his DNA sequence. We should have it on file if he's been around. If that won't work, I may need a new sample," Patterson required.

"Compton has been in prison so his DNA should be on file. If not, or there's a problem, let me know and I'll file a motion to get it. I'll have an investigator get the board to you tomorrow. What do you think the turnaround will be?"

"Could be six weeks, maybe more, depending on what we find and, if we need a new sample, how fast you can get his DNA to me. I'll let you know. Good to hear from you."

"I'm not sure if six weeks will work with the trial scheduled in two months. Any chance I can get this expedited?"

Spencer knew that he could get it expedited, if he went to Herald with a special request, but hoped to avoid that and an explanation of what he was doing. Herald would also not be too happy about burning a favor with the lab, if he could avoid it.

"Sure. I'll move it up. At least I can get you on my list. I'll get a little grumble soup here, but the techs will get over it for a good cause and all, and I like the idea of you owing me one," Patterson said with a laugh.

Spencer felt he had made progress in the right direction, but there was a nagging thought that DNA from an unknown could confound the case more than any defense attorney could, and it would all be on Spencer. That was the chance he was willing to take, and it might cost him his job, if it all went to hell. Then again, no one expected him to win the Compton case anyway so he should get some credit for ingenuity and effort that might save his bacon.

Chapter Twelve

That night Spencer settled in with the McBride trial transcript. It was a good diversion from his concerns about the risks in the Compton trial. Spencer's apartment had everything he needed to be comfortable and could not help making a comparison between what he had and what Molly lived with. Both had the same basics, but Spencer had a bedroom and a new easy chair that folded out into a comfortable lounger. He had several other chairs at a simple dinette that were modern by comparison and there was no smell of stale tobacco or the sense that he had not cleaned his apartment for a month. Later he may even cook spaghetti and the smell of an Italian kitchen would fill the room. He knew there was nothing like that expected at Molly's apartment. For entertainment, his television was a modern flat screen three times the size of Molly's and with cable for hundreds of channels. From what he could see, Molly only had local channels with a rabbit ear antenna. All told, he now had more appreciation for his few belongings and Molly's pitiful life.

The McBride case did not qualify as entertainment, but he believed the work of others on both sides would at least be interesting, especially since his boss was a leading participant for the State. There were hundreds of pages of motions and jury selection that Spencer decided to pass on for the time being and went directly to the trial, beginning with the opening statement of Prosecutor Herald. His statement was like watching a movie.

It had everything – sex, lust, murder, and intense expressions of emotion. Spencer was impressed at how Herald always repeated word pictures in several different ways as he moved through the story of how McBride stalked, raped, and murdered his victim. At the end Spencer knew that the jury could pass a pop quiz on any detail of the crime, and Herald left the jury with the assurance of proof beyond any doubt on the validity of the evidence to come.

The defense opening was less enthusiastic or promising. Alan Hoskins was an experienced defense attorney and, as often happens with single issue cases such as proof of identity, he put his best effort into challenging McBride's confession prior to trial. When that failed, his effort to challenge other evidence was diminished, leaving him to try to poke holes in the meaning and admissibility of other evidence. To Hoskins, the defense was hopeless regarding guilt, and his only hope was convincing just one juror to vote against the death penalty, that would take it off the table. With the prosecutor making no offer of life and a client that would not plead guilty; he felt he had nothing to lose. Of course, he could have opted for a trial before a three-judge panel, but with the political implications for them that would only be a guilty plea and execution in slow motion. No chance there.

Spencer kept a yellow legal pad at hand to take notes and to help keep track of the evidence introduced. There was a running evidence list with the transcript showing when an exhibit was first introduced and admitted into evidence, but he wanted to keep track himself to stay focused.

As Spencer read on, he could see that the evidence of guilt was overwhelming. Herald set the stage with the discovery of the body of Miss Stewart by calling her co-worker who had missed her at work. They were also friends. She not only expected Miss Stewart to be at work, but for her to call if she was not coming in. The co-worker's phone calls went unanswered, so she stopped by and found Miss Stewart's door unlocked and slightly ajar. As she entered and called out for Miss Stewart, nothing seemed disturbed, so she went back to the bedroom. It was there that she found Miss Stewart naked below the waist, on her bed, lifeless and covered in blood. It was not like the movies, she said. She didn't scream. She didn't cry. She was stunned and in shock at what she saw. She backed out of the room trembling and, after fumbling with her cell phone, called 911.

Next came the police who cautiously stepped in to preserve the scene. There had not been an immediate determination that a murder had taken place, but there were obvious injuries to the neck of Miss Stewart that reasonably suggested strangulation was the immediate cause of death, and by one strong enough to commit such an act. There were no open wounds. With the amount of blood on her lower torso, exsanguination could not be ruled out and consideration was also given to a violent rape either by penile penetration or by some object. Although no speculation on the manner and cause of death was offered by the first responders, the coroner later filled in those blanks with opinions that strangulation was the cause of death during a rape. It was a Tuesday, March 2, 1982, and Miss Stewart was seen at work the day before, so the detectives knew for certain that she was murdered sometime after she left work and arrived home. That at least narrowed time considerations.

The detectives who were called as witnesses detailed their efforts, standard in such a case, by canvassing the apartment complex as quickly as possible. Times, dates and places fade quickly in the minds of witnesses, so speed and accuracy are essential. During this process, two neighbors recounted seeing a young man, identified as McBride both in a photo line-up and in court, as being a visitor to the apartment of Miss Stewart on several occasions including on the date she was murdered.

The crime scene detectives testified to their cautious approach to processing Miss Stewart's apartment. It was essential that the scene was not contaminated by anyone not associated with the investigation and collection of evidence. While they were in the apartment it was sealed off from the inside out and a list was kept of anyone involved, both coming and going. In 1982, DNA had not yet been developed as an investigative tool, but there were other ways problems could be caused. One of the detectives' worst fears was finding a mystery fingerprint or even a hair that could not be identified as coming from a suspect, only to find after an acquittal that the supposed unknown and unidentified mystery perpetrator was just a nosy police officer who contaminated the scene during the investigation. To this extent and with the tools they had, the detectives were meticulous. Their first step was to photograph everything in the apartment without moving anything, including Miss Stewart. They did this as quickly as possible knowing that the County Coroner would be arriving soon and would need to do an on-scene gross examination of the body. That is, the body was face up and would simply be examined for anything immediately visible concerning injuries before an autopsy would be performed at the morgue. The body would also have to be turned over by the coroner at the scene to take a rectal temperature that may aid in the timing of her death and that entire process was documented and photographed. While not perfectly accurate for determining the time of a death, it is well established that the temperature of a body will drop at a specific rate depending on outside air temperature, but a number of other factors such as the normal living temperature of the deceased play into that result, so there are limitations on that calculation.

While the detectives were present, the County Coroner arrived with her assistant and proceeded to take duplicate photographs more limited to the body and immediate area. Spencer noted that they were both observed by the detectives putting on their blue nitrile gloves and that the assistant asked if the blue nitrile glove on the floor near the body was from one of the detectives. One of the detectives testified that it was not and would be collected as evidence after it was looked at by an on-scene technician checking for prints or anything apparent on the fingers such as blood. Spencer immediately concluded that McBride used gloves to eliminate fingerprints even though his fingerprints were found in her apartment. The detective also made the same conclusion and testified that the assumption was that the glove had been worn by the murderer which drew an immediate objection from the defense that was sustained with no further comment, but with the obvious damage done. Those are the bells in any trial that can never be forgotten and no motion for a mistrial was made by the defense with an afterthought. McBride always admitted he was at her apartment from time to time and finding his fingerprints would be no surprise, so why wear gloves in the first place? It was a logical argument, but one that fell on deaf ears of the jury as nothing more than defense spin.

A smart defense attorney always admits what cannot be refuted and he had to admit McBride had been at the apartment at least in the recent past. As with everything else, the glove was tagged, bagged and secured as evidence. The next witnesses were the medical experts, beginning with the County Coroner and pathologist who confirmed that strangulation was the cause of death that occurred while Miss Stewart was being violently raped with a great amount of consequential blood loss.

For one night's reading, Spencer had had enough, and it was time to call it quits. What he had read so far gave him confidence that Molly was simply wrong about her son and the alibi she tried to give him. It gave him additional confidence that nothing Molly could have said would have changed the end result – death by lethal injection. Even so, Spencer appreciated the logical mental process of Hoskins concerning the blue nitrile glove found. Just as Hoskins had suggested in his opening statement, McBride was no stranger to her and why would he bring gloves to Miss Stewart's apartment even if his primary motivation was to kill her? He had to know his prints would be found somewhere, as they were on the refrigerator, and there was no apparent attempt to wipe them off. As these thoughts filtered in, Spencer began to feel more like a defense attorney and less like an assistant prosecutor. Just the same, he considered his past as an asset to seeing through spurious defenses which he himself had at one time or another considered and made on behalf of an undeserving client. For now, he had to repress any notion that McBride was innocent.

With these thoughts, Spencer went to bed early. No late news. No late show or late- late show. He just wanted to get away from the review he brought upon himself, especially before he got to the autopsy of Miss Stewart. Now sleep, as always, would be his best friend and distraction.

Chapter Thirteen

The next day Spencer had to be in court early and, as predicted, Molly was waiting just outside the court room. Just as she looked up and was taking what appeared to be a deep breath, Spencer stopped her short with a sudden greeting of his own.

"Hello, Mrs. McBride. I have to get into the court room, but I would like to talk to you. I have a few questions and..."

"You know I'll be here."

It was the first time Spencer was not called a murderer. It may have been progress or she may have just been interrupted, but he was relieved. Just before noon Spencer came out and Molly was waiting. She said nothing, but Spencer again greeted her and apologized for taking so long.

"Mrs. McBride, I have started reading your son's trial transcript and a few things came up that maybe you can clear up. What kind of work was you son doing when he was arrested?"

"He wasn't doing anything. He didn't have any steady job. People liked him like the Stewart lady and would give him odd jobs, but nothing steady."

"Did he ever have any rubber gloves in any work he did."

"The police asked me about blue rubber gloves. I never used any and Billy didn't either."

"But how do you know that? They can be bought anywhere. There is really nothing special about them."

"Maybe not for you. I never heard Billy ever talk about rubber gloves and never saw him wearing any. And besides what little money Billy had he would not be spending on rubber gloves no matter what the color."

That had a ring of truth to it. No one buys a pair of blue nitrile gloves. Spencer knew they are sold by the box and no box of rubber gloves or the other glove – if there was one – was ever found.

"So, what's going on with the glove now?" Molly asked.

"Nothing, really. It was just something that was found where the murder occurred. I don't think it had anything to do with the case other than raise questions about why it was there. Only one glove was found, and I suppose it could also have belonged to Miss Stewart. It's just a part of the case that I really don't understand."

"Are you going to find out?" Molly asked in a way that suggested a sign of hope.

Giving her any hope, Spencer thought, would be a mistake with the execution not far off. Curiosity though, of which Spencer always had an abundance, is different than hope and he needed to stay on track with his one and only objective to relieve the guilt Molly was carrying from her botched testimony resulting in the upcoming execution of her only son.

"I'm just curious, Mrs. McBride. I suppose you could say the case against your son does fit like a glove and then there is this damn glove that fits the case in some ways and not in others."

Spencer did not go into detail, but he knew that in every case juries are faced with some evidence that doesn't make sense. Both sides in every case are faced with the challenge of rewriting history, as they see it and, just like history, some evidence cannot be explained. That by itself does not create reasonable doubt. Doubt, yes, but not reasonable doubt. Those are the problems juries face every day while trying to reach a verdict, and eventually reason and common sense win out to fill in the blanks, even if the unexplained have to take a back seat in the process to reach a verdict. It is that part of the system of justice that bothered Spencer. To him, a finding of guilt required perfection and that was not a part of the law of reasonable doubt. Whether it's a horseshoe or a glove, it has to fit with no room for error. Although he hated the cliché "if it doesn't fit, you must acquit", popular in defense circles, he agreed with the principle even as an assistant prosecutor.

"Are you going to do anything about it? Isn't it too late?"

"You're right and I apologize for thinking out loud. I suppose the jury had the same questions and I am sure the police did everything to find out if the glove was significant."

"I don't believe it. I don't think they did a very good job. They only wanted to convict Billy and you all got that done. Murderers. You are all a bunch of murderers. What do you want from me?" Molly asked with anguish pouring out as she began to cry openly.

"Nothing. I am just trying to understand so you will understand and not blame yourself or me for what is going to happen," he said without mentioning the ultimate penalty facing Billy.

"Don't do me any favors. You're just like everyone else. Just leave me alone, but don't count on me leaving you alone. You and all the rest of you," as more hate and anger filled her words.

"I'll do my best to leave you alone, but if I don't, you may end up hating me anyway for it and that's I risk I'll take, OK?"

Molly didn't answer. Spencer had not counted on telling her why he was getting involved and he did just the same even though Molly probably could not understand it. Now through her tears, he was all in and there would be no turning back until he was satisfied the jury got it right or got it wrong. There would be no in between. The glove seemed like the first and best place to start and that would take him back to Central Records. Spencer already had a lot on his plate. The Compton case was coming up; he needed to stay focused on that. With any luck the processing of the board would solve that, but he could not rely on that outcome. Still, he could look at the evidence in the McBride case, and suddenly he felt the need to consider the deadline. If the jury got it right, Molly would have to live with it and understand that there was nothing she could have done to change the outcome. If Spencer found the jury got it wrong, he knew his world would be turned upside down and time was running out. Suddenly he became a timekeeper for Billy's execution and wished there was a simple way out without feeling like a coward. There were no options except to press on and like his father always said: "Never quit unless you have to, and the 'have to' part is up to your conscience and the Almighty." Spencer always said his father never did him any favors with that one.

Chapter Fourteen

The next day Spencer was able to avoid his usual morning dose of Molly and went straight to his office to continue pulling together trial materials on the Compton case. Of course, if his hunch panned out, he would be looking at that case in the rear-view mirror of closed cases, but he was far from counting on that. When he arrived, his secretary told him Herald wanted to see him, so he made his way to Herald's office without delay.

"Good morning, Ann. I was told the Boss wants to see me."

"He does. It will just be a few minutes. He's talking to one of the Commissioners about our budget, but I don't think it will be too long. I think his attention span on math issues is a little limited."

"Mine, too," Spencer said, hoping that the subject would not put Herald in a foul mood.

It wasn't long before Herald signaled his secretary to send Spencer in and she gave him a gesture to go right in.

"Good morning, Tallbridge. I hear you are working hard and doing good work, but there are a couple of things coming up and you need to be aware of potential problems. Someone mentioned, and I don't remember who, that you have been talking to Molly McBride."

Spencer listened intently and hoped that it was limited to what someone observed with his hallway meeting with Molly.

Fortunately, that turned out to be the case. Who told Herald was another question that would remain unanswered, but Spencer figured it was probably Arnold.

"I know it's disconcerting, to say the least, to be called a murderer in the hallways around here by Molly McBride. We put up with it. I put up with it and so do the Judges. I could do something about it, but the press would pick it up and suddenly I'm in the papers or worse, in court on a free speech beef. I don't need that. In a couple of months it should all be over, with the execution. What I am concerned about is you talking to her and giving her some kind of ammunition to delay the execution. That did happen once before when DNA first came out and one of my now former assistants told her about it, no doubt feeling sorry for her and her never ending claim that her son is innocent. It put the execution off for years. They are all scheduled way in advance and any delay is monumental, not minor, to the schedule. Do you see where I'm going?"

"Yes, sir."

"OK, just so we have a clear understanding, what's your understanding?" Herald asked.

"Molly is going to get us, me, in trouble, if I'm not careful, so it is best if I just ignore her and put up with her rant."

"Thank you. I think we have a perfect understanding. Now tell me, how do you like being an assistant prosecutor?"

"I like it fine. Except for Molly McBride, it's everything I'd hoped for and maybe more. It's great to have the full weight of the state on my side, you know, the labs, the technicians, the police, the experts and the money to pay them. I have everything I need to do my job and a far cry from what I had."

"Are you telling me you were more resourceful as a defense attorney?"

"I suppose in a way I had to do all my own thinking on a tight budget and now instead of just being a musician, I get to be a director, if you know what I mean."

"I think so. I never really thought about it in musical terms, but the power of the state, what we have available, is almost beyond comprehension. Even so, we still lose cases."

Spencer wanted to correct him and say that the losses might sometimes be from bad facts beyond any power of the state to change, but this was not the time to debate the issue.

"I know you have the Compton trial coming up, but I will be attending the McBride execution and I will need someone to drive me up. If you're interested, I can get a seat for you, too. I do think it is an experience that every assistant prosecutor should have."

Spencer knew there could be only one answer.

"Yes, sir," Spencer said. "I'll be happy to drive you up and look forward to it. I agree that seeing an execution instead of just reading the pundits the next day will be invaluable. I hope I can make good company for you and it should give us a lot to talk about; that is, if you are interested in talking about the death penalty."

"Of course, and we will plan on it, if your other case doesn't get in the way. Keep me in the loop, OK?"

"Yes, sir," Spencer said without hesitation.

After the meeting with Herald, Spencer went back to his office, shut the door and began to assess what he had just gotten himself into. Was it a problem or a blessing? Was this his way out or was there unfinished business he promised himself even if he had made no direct promise or commitment to Molly to review her son's case. Once again, he sensed that he was grinding and grinding into the quick. He just had not felt the pain yet, but he knew that if he continued as he had planned, the pain would come and maybe the loss of his job. "Time for another call to Dad?" he questioned to himself. "No," he concluded. This was something he needed to do on his own, at least for now. He knew the penalty. Herald made it clear that he was on shaky ground walked on by a now "former assistant prosecutor". Being fired was the price and, considering the trouble that a former assistant prosecutor caused by delaying an execution date, it would be a price assuredly paid if he was caught helping Molly again. Spencer never saw anyone from the prosecutor's office while talking to Molly, but it would only have taken a momentary distraction to miss someone taking in his discussion with Molly, and again he was left with Herald's admonition that there were no secrets in the courthouse.

That night Spencer decided to review the post-trial motion in the McBride case about DNA. It was the basis for a delay in one of the many execution dates and was one of those not usually expected and granted. Execution dates are first set with awareness that the date is more like a suggestion. While required to be set as a definite date, everyone knows that the appeals process and other court challenges call for seemingly endless resetting of the final date and result in 25% of all those sentenced to death nationally to die of old age. In the McBride case, DNA was a new science not in existence at the time of the trial. That new science took the place of new evidence and triggered hundreds of post appeals and delays to give science a chance, as opposed to the finality of an execution. When it was suggested that DNA might clear McBride in spite of his confession and the failure of his alibi, the court was unwilling to let it pass without questioning such exacting proof. Spencer had not reviewed McBride's confession, but it had been ruled admissible by a Judge and reviewed by others on the many appeals that followed. Even if the confession was flawed in one or many ways, it would make no difference now as it had been considered as well as the issue of DNA all the way to the United States Supreme Court.

That night when Spencer got home, he could not think about the Compton case. He was totally distracted by the McBride case and what, if anything might have been missed. The lab results from the DNA exam of all the physical evidence turned up nothing except McBride's DNA on the refrigerator and the DNA of the victim. The lab report on the glove only showed it was used in the murder because her DNA was on it and the folded over inside of the glove cuff showed nothing on reexamination from the swabs taken. "How was that possible?" Spencer questioned. If the glove was worn, wouldn't there be DNA on the inside of the cuff? There would be, he thought, unless the killer wore a long sleeve shirt that covered the cuff. That would explain the absence of DNA from the wrist of the killer. Spencer read the report over and over, convinced that he had missed something. He felt it but didn't know what it was until he thought the words, "I just can't put my finger on it." And there it was. For Spencer it was a eureka moment – that seldom-felt solution – that comes out of the blue and bites you in the ass saying, "Here I am." There was no reported swab of the inside fingers of the glove all the way down to the tip. There had to be DNA there, he thought, and it should be tested. But how?

Spencer had a monumental problem. Sure, he could tell Herald of his bright idea and get fired. He could go ahead and get fired and there was no one that would listen. The Innocence Project might pick it up for retesting and a last-minute call for a Supreme Court delay, but that was a long shot and it would torture Molly in the process. After all, everything had been tested, and there was the possibility that the lab would quickly say that the finger, inside and out, was tested as a matter of protocol even though there was no mention of an inside examination. All that, however, was unlikely because Herald had signed off on sending the glove swabs for retesting and no one considered sending the glove.

Spencer soon concluded that there was no safe way out. There could be evidence that would convince the world of McBride's guilt and to find it Spencer would risk getting fired or worse, although he was not quite sure what worse might be. But he had a feeling deep down that any solution might be illegal. It was time for a break. He needed to get away from himself but was having a hard time doing it. His sense of logic toward a solution was taking hold and he needed to make it fit. He started his mental process in the comfort of what he knew. He knew he had a glove, but did he? The first thing he had to know is whether or not the glove was still in existence. All the evidence in the case had been returned to Rutledge County following the final appeal so it should still be held in Central Records. Then what? So, if and when he finds it, he questioned, what's next? There would be no way to have it examined without bringing the courthouse down on himself. There was that damn glove with five chances for DNA of McBride and perhaps someone else, which was a secondary thought only remotely considered in a momentary daydream of unlikely courtroom heroics. Still, there needed to be an answer and the second step was eluding him until he took another break in the process to think about the Compton case and the possible timing conflict with McBride's execution. It was in making that connection that he began to turn the corner from being an ethical, honest, assistant prosecutor and attorney to someone worthy of being disbarred and perhaps charged with a crime.

He would use the Compton case. DNA was being sent up for testing and why not include a few swabs of DNA samples from the inside fingers of the glove, assuming it could be found. It was an intriguing thought. McBride's DNA would also be on file, but the lab would only be looking to include Compton's DNA or exclude it. The lab would have no need to go looking for the identity of any mystery DNA, if it wasn't Compton's. The only question was whether or not it was his. Of course, Spencer couldn't ask it to be compared with McBride's because that would bring the house down so he would have to somehow include Molly's DNA. Maternal DNA from Molly was a sure test of relationship even without Billy's sample. Her DNA, as his mother, would have a unique signature identifying Billy. It would not be a perfect match, but close enough. All he would have to do is send swabs, five from the inside fingers and one from Molly, as hitch hikers for DNA testing in the Compton case and hope for the best. His expectation was that the five swabs would all match, with Molly's being a very close match, and that would convince anyone, including Molly, that McBride deserved his fate regardless of any argument on the penalty itself. The worst that could happen, if he were caught and it was Billy's, is that he would be fired for corrupting evidence in a case and have a lot of explaining to do. That championed the principle that the ends justified his means. No harm, no foul. Then again, if it was McBride's and no one discovered the deceptions he practiced, Spencer alone would have to live with his own conscience. There would also be a lab report about the hitchhiking DNA, and Spencer concluded he would have to be attentive to intercept the report from ever seeing the light of day and make a good cover story about its inclusion in the Compton case, if discovered. On the remote possibility it wasn't Billy's, he would have to step up. Of course, he would still be fired, but at least an innocent man would not be put to death, and he was willing to risk his future on that. There was also the possibility that no DNA would be found and solve everything for him as having done the best he could. On a risk benefit basis, Spencer liked the plan and needed to put it in motion at the first opportunity. That might take some doing to examine and swab the glove, if it could even be found.

The next day Spencer went back to Central Records and asked about the evidence in the McBride case.

"Hello again, Ms. Renner," Spencer greeted the clerk. "I need to take a look at evidence in the McBride case and I'm hoping you can help me out."

"Sure. It's 'Laura' by the way. Couldn't get what you needed from the transcript?"

"Not really. There was a lot of testimony about photographs, and I think seeing those will prove, as usual, that a photograph really is worth a thousand words."

"I have to be with you when you take a look. I am not supposed to let anyone review evidence without supervision."

"That's OK. Do you have the time to do it now or should I come back later?"

"Now works for me. I'll get the key and we will take a look."

Spencer watched as the records clerk went to her desk and pulled out the short stick with several keys attached. No doubt one was for the evidence locker he was looking for.

"Just follow me," she said happily and led him to the second floor.

"Did you bring gloves?" she asked. "I have some and you will have to wear them during any examination, but you probably knew that."

"No. I'll have to use yours, sorry." He didn't know the procedure and did not have his own with him, although he kept a box of them in his briefcase at his office. His answer took care of both questions without telling her how inexperienced he was with the procedure.

"That's fine. We keep them up there anyway."

At the second floor, the clerk went to a large standing cabinet. She told Spencer at his first visit that she was familiar with the McBride case and knew where to look. Based on the procedure the clerk required, Spencer quickly realized that it might be a problem doing anything more than looking for, and hopefully finding, the glove. Making any test in the presence of the clerk would be impossible unless he could distract her long enough, and that would take some planning. He decided first things first.

Find the glove and then work out the testing problem later. There was no urgency, just another hurdle if he found the glove. The prospect of breaking in after-hours was only a brief consideration as he noted the location of the keys to the evidence lockers. Inside the cabinet, a box of gloves was readily available, and a large notice read that nothing was to be touched without gloves worn. As expected, the gloves were the standard issue for investigations – blue nitrile. The clerk found a large banker's box with the name and number of the McBride case and lifted it out. She carried it to an empty room the size of a small office with a long table to lay things out.

"So here you are. Do you want me to sort through the evidence for the photographs?"

"No, I can do it," and Spencer began to lift out envelops with descriptions of contents and stopped when he found one marked "Photographs".

"I need to look at these and they might be grisly so you might not want to watch."

"We see graphic stuff here all the time. It's no big deal. I hope you don't mind, but we are shorthanded today…"

Spencer broke in, "I can come back if you need to leave. I can make an appointment that will work for you."

"No. It's OK. I just have to go downstairs. We don't get a lot of traffic, but someone has to watch the door. You're an assistant prosecutor, and if I can't trust you who can I trust."

"Thank you for your trust," Spencer said, feeling more like a criminal than an attorney and wishing that he had Buccal kits with him to get the sampling over with. There were close to 50 photographs of the crime scene and a few showed the same blue nitrile glove incidental to the general crime scene.

"Just don't mention it."

"You can count on that and thanks," Spencer said as she left the floor.

Now he quickly moved on, looking for the envelope with the glove. He needed to find it, examine it and do it all before the clerk returned. It wasn't long before he found an envelope with the description of the glove, and he carefully opened the envelope and shook out the contents without touching it. His immediate observation was that the glove looked exactly like the glove pictured in the photograph and mentioned in the transcript, including the fold at the wrist. It did not appear to have been turned any more inside out than what was pictured and there was nothing to indicate that the inside had ever been tested, except the cuff, as noted in the DNA lab report. For Spencer a test of each finger inside the glove was now in play, and he just needed the time and privacy to get it done. Spencer quickly put the glove back in the envelope and put everything back into the evidence box. Now was the time for the next deception in his plan and he went looking for the clerk.

"Looks like I have to leave. Just got a call, so I just put everything back in the box. I feel bad that I didn't finish, but it will be a good excuse to come back for a visit. Thanks for your help. I hate to bother you when you're short staffed. How often does that happen?"

"Flattery always works around here," the clerk said with obvious humor. "Come back anytime. The other clerk is usually off on Tuesdays and I usually go to lunch at twelve thirty. We are not too busy before noon and I will look forward to helping out."

"Just what I needed to hear." Spencer tossed off the gloves into a trash can. He could not help but notice that the fold of the glove after taking it off of his right hand almost matched perfectly with the glove he examined. Now he had a plan and an unwitting clerk to move on to the next level. He just needed to arrive back before the clerk's lunch when she was busy and short staffed.

Chapter Fifteen

Later that afternoon, Spencer stopped at the Sheriff's Department on the pretext of talking about the Compton case.

"Hello, Jake," Spencer said to the lead detective Jake Butler. "Thanks for getting that board in the Compton case to the lab. During the trial I'll be talking a lot about DNA test procedures. Do you have any of the swab kits you can give me? I need some for demonstrative purposes with the jury."

"Sure. How many. You mean Buccal kits, right?"

"Right. Six will be more than enough and I will hold on to the ones I don't use for the next time."

"No problem," Jake said enthusiastically and handed a handful of at least six to Spencer.

This hurdle went better than expected. Spencer also told his first major lie, but so far, he held firm to his rationalization that 'no harm, no foul' justified what he was doing. He would take his deception one step at a time, rationalizing all the way that he had not done anything illegal so far, but his conscience was not as clear.

Back at his office, Spencer took a close look at the Buccal kits and considered what he would have to do. He causally shut his door after telling his secretary that he had to do some reading on the Compton case and laid the Buccal tests out on his desk. In each kit was a Q-tip swab inside a small glass vial about the size of a test tube. It was sealed tightly, and a simple set of instructions was included. It was apparent that the test was designed to be used on a wet surface such as the inside wall of a mouth, and the inside of the glove would no doubt be dry. To use the test kit effectively, he would probably have to wet the Q-tip, but he needed to know how that is actually done was an unknown; it needed to be known. Patterson ought to be able to supply that answer and Spencer made the call.

"Hello, Agent. It's Spencer Tallbridge down in Rutledge."

"Hi, Spencer. What can I do for you? I hope you're not in a rush on that board you sent up."

"No, I was just wondering how you try to extract DNA from something old and really dry?" Spencer felt that was an honest question that had everything to do with the Compton case, which gave him the feeling of cover from his less than forthright purpose.

"Sure. We use the same Buccal kits that you are familiar with for cheek swabs except we maintain sterility. We use a standard sterile solution. Well, not really a solution. That implies that there is more to the liquid than just water. It's distilled water and it is lab tested to eliminate any possible contamination from the person distilling it. Does that make sense?"

"Perfect sense. So, you don't just go to the grocery store and get a jug of distilled water you use for ironing your shirts," Spencer said with a laugh.

"That's right. You probably could use a medical-grade eyewash that you get at the drug store because it is supposed to be certified pure, but we have no control over that. We get ours from a supplier, and we run our own tests. Good questions, though, to make a point with a jury about how careful we are. You know we can do swabs here when you need something tested. There's no need for your detectives to do it."

"Well, I was just wondering about a dry surface like the board. I also think there may be a few more swabs that the police want examined, just to eliminate any unknowns at the crime scene, like police and investigators who might have left some of their DNA behind inadvertently. I'll be sending those, and I'll get them up to you ASAP and give you a call. I think there might be a cigarette butt from a detective, and I'll make sure it's marked for you to do DNA testing on it along with the rest."

"Great, no need to call. Just be sure to have them sent to my attention since I am working on the case and I'll know what you're after. Try to get those to me sooner than later, OK?"

"You got it. Thanks again."

Spencer got exactly what he needed from Patterson and made a quick stop at the local Paramount Drug Store to see what was available in the eyewash department. It made sense that eyewash would be clean of anything but the purist liquid, hopefully just water, to wash the sensitive tissues of eyes. Hopefully the label would tell, and it did. Most of the products qualified as "medicated" and that would not work. He needed pure, non-medicated wash and he found just one that fit that requirement. Just the same, when Spencer got it home, he gave it two tests. The first was a taste test and it seemed just like advertised. The second was an eye test. He used two drops in each eye and felt nothing but wet. He knew there was nothing scientific about what he was doing, and he took on faith and his amateur testing that any DNA, if in the glove, would not be contaminated or destroyed by him. Next he needed one more experiment. Just how long would it take to get four samples? It would take time to put on gloves; it would take time to arrange the test vials. It would take time to use each of the four Q-tips, and it would take time to put everything back as found before the records clerk returned, if he could even get that time alone. How long would it take was the ultimate question assuming no slips or interruptions? Maybe he should just steal the evidence package when Laura was distracted and do it all at his apartment. But he knew that once the evidence left Central Records it would be considered corrupted and that was a nonstarter. Getting caught in the process was also not an option.

Spencer took a letter envelope and put a nitrile glove into it, recreating as best he could remember where the fold of the glove was, and put it in an empty box close to the size of the evidence box where the glove to be tested was located. He looked at his watch and silently said, "Go". Because of the requirement of the records clerk, he would already have on gloves so no time would be lost there. His first step would be to reach into the box and pull out the envelope with the glove. He decided not to remove the glove from the envelope immediately and proceeded to take out the Buccal kits from his suit coat pocket and set them on the table where he was timing the test. Next, he took out the eyewash and found that there would be a lot of wasted time in opening each kit to put a drop of wash on each tip. That would be best solved by wetting each Q-tip before he arrived, so he re-started the time with that assumption. Mentally, Spencer said the necessary stages to himself. "Get envelope from evidence box, open envelope, take each test kit one at a time and remove and wet each Q-tip and swab each one in and to the full length of each finger, close each vial, replace glove into evidence envelope, put envelope back into evidence box, put vials in coat and let clerk know he was leaving. Mission accomplished." He checked the time. If it went as planned, he could get it all done in two minutes and thirty-five seconds. How to label each kit would be the next consideration, but that could be done later, and he was not concerned about which vial went with which finger with all the fingers being tested. Suddenly, one thought came to mind that covered one base not considered so far. If McBride's DNA was not on any of the five samples, just how was he supposed to prove that, having swabbed out all the fingers? The solution was easy. Leave one untouched, and it wouldn't matter which one. The only question remaining was whether or not McBride's DNA was on any of the test kits. Now he had a plan. All he need-ed was an opportunity.

Chapter Sixteen

When Spencer arrived at the Prosecutor's office the next day there were cameras and film crews outside Herald's office. That was not unusual to keep the locals informed. Herald often gave interviews on pending cases.

"What's it about today?" Spencer asked his secretary.

"I think it's about the McBride execution coming up. They start coverage early and they get his view of the death penalty to compare and contrast again with the defense opinions and the bleeding hearts. We've been through this several times and I think Herald uses the same old scripts he has used in the past. He has plenty of them."

"Do you have any idea when it will air?" Spencer asked.

"Probably tonight, but this will be just the beginning. He likes to build a little tension now and raise the level or take it to a new level the closer we get to the execution date. It keeps him in the news, if you know what I mean."

"I do. It's his job and I guess there is an element of theater to all this."

"Very perceptive," she noted as she handed him a number of discovery requests from defense attorneys on new cases. "How's the social life going? None of my business really, but you seem to be working a lot lately."

"I'm fine. I want to make a good impression. You probably know the drill."

"I do, but there aren't any football heroes around here to get in the way."

"Ouch!" Spencer was surprised she remembered a sour note in his love life such as it was.

"How do you think your life would have been different if you were a football hero?"

"Wow, that's a tough one. I never really considered that," Spencer said and did his best to avoid opening up about his past relationship that ended so poorly.

"I think it would have ended the same way. They were what you might call childhood sweethearts and I wasn't. Even a soulmate has a hard time overcoming that. I just missed the boat and probably didn't do enough to get on board. I blame myself. As you joked it was a good case of sour dough for me and not for her. Now I'm just not looking for another boat ride and I'm doing my best to just stay afloat around here. Looking back is not healthy anyway, but thanks for asking." He hoped to put an end to her relevant enquiries with his shipwreck metaphors.

"Where is she now?"

"Wooster," Spencer said flatly without elaboration.

"That explains a lot, but I'm still looking out for you. All you single assistant prosecutors have a lot to offer and it will be fun to see how it all works out for you, if you are around that long without leaving for greener pastures. I still think you could use a friend, like maybe a dog."

"Enough said. Thanks for the optimism and suggestion," Spencer said as he left the room and ruminating that just maybe the non-fraternization rule was a bad idea.

That night Spencer went to the TV to check the early news to see Herald's interview. Sure enough, there he was as serious as a heart attack, grimly telling how important it was for justice to be served by the execution of Billy McBride.

"This has gone on far too long. Justice delayed is justice denied," Herald exclaimed. Spencer had heard that same argument over the years, and it had a ring of truth to it that compared well with his view for the need of quick and sure justice. The only consideration was the possibility of mistakes from bad evidence such as mistaken identities and coached or lying witnesses, but those were few and far between and usually taken care of by the way the system actually worked slowly and deliberately. Nevertheless, it was good politics for Herald to complain about the delays in the McBride execution and this one was certain to take place in a month.

Herald took the opportunity again, to extol the painstaking investigation and the help of Arnold, now his Chief of the criminal division. Arnold kept out of the limelight, and always appreciated a word of praise from Herald concerning his work, especially on death penalty cases. He had always been Herald's right-hand man from the beginning and assumed the heavy lifting of the day to day activities of the office.

One of the reporters asked Herald what he expected to gain from executing McBride after all these years of delays and false starts and his answer was to the point. "It will deter McBride. That's all I need to know. Who knows if it will deter others? If it does, so much the better, but I want to deter him and that's all you need to know. What he did to that girl is beyond redemption. Case closed. I do not want to breathe the same air he breathes. His is a life that should never have been conceived in the first place and we will all be far better off without him. That's what I call deterrence."

It was a perfect sound bite for Herald from years of training on how to say a lot in just a few words that would resonate with those favoring the death penalty. Those he always assumed were in the majority and the rest did not matter to him. There was no counterpoint from McBride's attorneys. They left the argument of vengeance and an eye for an eye to Herald. No doubt they were busy planning another last-minute motion for another stay, and nothing would be gained from more public debate on the death penalty. Spencer felt, however, that the time for another stay had long since passed and even if anything is possible in the ever-changing world of the United States Supreme Court, the door to that Court was probably tightly closed.

"You have a call from an old friend. Do you want to take it?" Spencer's secretary asked.

"Old friend? Who is it?" Spencer asked in disbelief.

"I asked, but he said, 'Just tell him it's an old friend.'"

"OK, I'll take it. Thanks," as Spencer picked up the phone. "Hello. This is Spencer Tallbridge. I was told you are an old friend. Surprise me."

"I'm not an old friend. I'm really an old retired detective, and I want to talk to you about something you are handling that has concerned me," the caller said with obvious stress in his voice by tripping over the words handling and concerned.

"Well, a name might be a good place to start and we can go from there."

"O.K; I'm Brent Prescott. My sister said you are looking at the McBride case, and I would like to talk to you about it."

"I remember your name from the McBride transcript. Is your sister Laura Renner?" Spencer asked hopefully.

"Yes. Her married name is Renner."

"What's the big secret with your name and the old friend line? Come on in and we can talk."

"I'm not so sure that's a good idea to be seen at your office. The last time I talked to one of you guys, he got canned and I caught a shit storm of trouble, but it's something still on my mind, if you're interested. If not, I understand and just forget I called."

"No, I want to talk to you. Where can we meet? Your call."

"Laura said you're a new hire. Are you from around here?"

"No, and I would like to stay around for a while. I'm not sure what you are getting me into, but I'm willing to listen."

"In that case it might be a good idea not to mention my name at least until you hear what I have to say. What does your schedule look like after you get off today?"

Spencer had planned on a visit to Central Records to put his plan in action and was feeling the pressure of delay starting to creep into his blueprint, but it would have to wait. His curiosity took hold and he needed to know what Prescott had to say. He also knew he would have to visit Molly in secret to hopefully get a cigarette butt from her for DNA testing and it was now becoming more complicated.

"I'm good after 5:00 P.M. Where do you want to meet?"

"Pick me up at the corner of Third and Main at 5:30 P.M. I'll be the guy with a red ball cap and sunglasses on the right side of Third Street. We'll find a place to talk from there."

"You're on. I have a white Ford Focus. It looks like every car on the market that's not an SUV. I'll honk a few times when I see you."

Now Spencer had another possible mystery on his hands to further complicate his life and leading him further into the quick.

Chapter Seventeen

Third and Main was fortunately easy to find and, as he approached, he could see a fellow with a red hat and glasses standing at the corner. He pulled over. There was no need to honk as Prescott quickly opened the door and got in. From there Prescott said nothing, not even an introduction, except to give further directions.

"Take the next right and go down to Victory Park. I think that will be private enough for what I have to say. I don't think anyone will recognize me there."

Spencer did as instructed and found that the parking lot was virtually empty. It was getting cold, fall was in the air and the sun set early, so few if any used the park at that time. It was a good place to be for whatever they had to talk about."

"So, what's on your mind with all this secret stuff?" Spencer asked.

"Nice to meet you, Spencer. My sister said you seemed like one of the good guys and she likes you. If she likes you, I like you and I don't want to get you in trouble."

"I can't imagine what that would be," Spencer replied, knowing full well that the McBride case was off limits for creating problems close to McBride's execution.

"Like I said on the phone, there was an assistant prosecutor who was looking into the McBride case before the last scheduled execution date for McBride and he screwed it up. I'm not sure how much I had to do with it. It may have been more about his contact with McBride's mother, but I did share a concern and it may have got him canned. Like I said on the phone, if this is something you don't want to get involved with, we can cut it right now and I'll walk."

"I think as an assistant prosecutor, I have to know, even if someone else might not think so."

Spencer did not explain his meaning by saying further that he would be at cross purposes with Herald, if he followed his conscience and asked Prescott to proceed.

"I wasn't a detective very long before I got dispatched to Linda Stewart's apartment. Other detectives were already there and I was given the detail of keeping the crime scene secure. Pretty easy job. I just had to know the players and separate the curious from the pros. I was there before the Coroner, and I did go inside briefly before I was told to secure the area. It was a bloody mess. One of the worst I've seen. It stays with you. I could tell she hand been strangled by the marks on her neck and there was dried blood that led back to her nose and mouth. The way it traced told me she was down while she was bleeding. The worst of what I saw was her exposed pubic area. Just from looking at all the blood there, I could tell that she had probably been raped, but all that was up to the coroner. There were no panties, but maybe she didn't wear any. Who knows? One thing that stood out to me was a blue rubber glove on the floor near her body, and it was a no brainer that it wasn't a part of our investigation team," Prescott noted.

"So, what's so unusual about finding evidence?" Spencer asked. "You saw it and so did everyone else. It was photographed, tagged and bagged. Later it was examined and years later it was examined again. What's the big deal with that rubber glove?" Spencer asked again knowing all the while that he was about to make a big deal about the glove that would clinch the case against McBride.

"At the time, I didn't think anything about it," Prescott explained. "I was just trying to be a good detective, and being observant was something my superiors stressed all the time. It's what makes a great detective; I wanted to be one. I wasn't entrusted with McBride's interrogation, but I knew the guys that were. They were always relentless. Later, around the squad, they would high five themselves about how they got McBride to confess. The interrogation trick with a weak mind or a young kid was to tell them that if they just told them what they wanted to know they could go home. It usually worked, but I always had a problem with that. Unless you really are guilty, I don't think most innocent people would fully comprehend the consequences of telling a false story and by then it's too late. Just the same, jurors think only guilty people confess and usually that is true. It's just the innocent ones that bother me after all these years."

"So, it's the confession that we are here about?" Spencer asked.

"No. Sorry I got started down that path. Several years later there was another homicide. It appeared to be a burglary gone bad and putting those two offenses together made it a death penalty case. It was nothing like the McBride case. No rape; just theft and death. This time I was more involved, and again before the Coroner got there a blue glove was on the floor near the body, and this is where you come in. It looked just like the McBride case as far as the glove was concerned and no one thought much of what I had to say. It just didn't feel right. I was always told that serial killers always leave something behind or save something from a murder as a souvenir and I thought the glove fit the 'left behind' thing. I thought the killer wanted to let us know there were no prints like the McBride case and McBride was in prison. Maybe I was too much into the detective thing, but I never believed in coincidences. I used to watch Kojak reruns. Maybe you remember him."

"I do. Perry Mason was my guys for reruns, but I get your point."

"One of his best lines that I always remembered was that he would rather eat a thousand rotten oysters than one coincidence. Not sure if you ever bit into a rotten oyster, but it is something you never forget. Talk about a rotten taste in your mouth. Any way, we eventually caught the guy and he also confessed like McBride. Like they all do he started out denying the whole thing, but we broke him."

"Did you have anything to do with that?" Spencer asked.

"Not the first round, but I did later, and he seemed anxious to tell us all about it."

"Did he give you anything that only the killer would know?"

"He did, but that changed at trial. There he said he was told things in the first round of questioning that was put together in his confession when I was there. I never believed we set him up. I didn't think we worked that way. The high five thing was for a job well done or so I thought at the time."

"Not so sure now? Is that what you're telling me?"

"Yes, but it's really about the glove. After he was convicted by Herald and given the death penalty, that new DNA stuff came out and his lawyers asked for an examination just like in the McBride case. I didn't pay much attention to that because they were all asking for it, even the ones seen on video murdering someone. That was always a hoot. We were told it was just for delay."

"So, what's your problem now?"

"I talked to an assistant in your office about the glove and my observation about the gloves in both cases. To me it was more than odd or a coincidence that a single blue nitrile glove would be found at two murders. Not two gloves. Just one. The assistant prosecutor started looking into it and it ramped up out of control. Before long I was being questioned about whether I even saw both gloves and whether they could have come from the Coroner. We knew the first wasn't true because there were pictures, but the second wasn't so clear. When they went to get it from evidence, it was gone and there was no record why. Your boss, Herald, was really pissed. He said it would screw up the execution like the McBride case, but it didn't, and the poor son-of-a-bitch was executed without any more concern about that glove. The assistant prosecutor wasn't fired but came close because of what another assistant did earlier to foul up the McBride case for a while. I didn't get fired either, but my chief thought I was a loon. I guess because I was told I was not thinking straight or a team player, I have always carried my question about that glove until my sister said you were reading the case for some reason. And I have to tell you if you let this conversation out, your days on Herald's staff will be numbered."

Spencer realized he had met someone who had been grinding for years and never got anywhere except a guilt trip on a case where an innocent man may have been executed.

"So how are you going to deal with it if an innocent man was executed?"

"I don't really know. I do know I will have to deal with it, and I really don't know if that's where you are going. I just need to get it out with someone that might make a difference one way or another."

That was the difference between Molly and Prescott. The truth would set him free with or without guilt and not so for Molly. Spencer had heard all that was necessary.

"Can you tell me what you're doing if you are doing anything about the McBride case?" Prescott asked.

Guardedly, Spencer said, "No. Whatever I do, you are better off not knowing and that does not mean I am doing anything at all."

With that cryptic response few words were spoken as Spencer started his car and dropped off Prescott off where he found him.

As Prescott got out of the car, he turned to Spencer and said, "Maybe it's that old detective intuition in me, but I have a feeling about you. We might never meet again but let me leave you with this. I'm counting on you to do the right thing. Fair enough?"

"Fair enough."

Chapter Eighteen

Spencer now thought he had a second person to cure from a bad history and that the resolution would probably not be the exoneration of McBride. On his way home he passed by a sign that read at first glance "Dog Pound" and then saw the complete name "Dog by the Pound". A novel title, he thought, and decided to take up Amy about the value of man's best friend. He stopped in to just look around and perhaps find one for Molly someday, if she needed a friend, too, as he expected it all to pan out. As he opened the door, it triggered a spring-loaded bell giving rise to a cacophony of dogs barking and birds singing to further announce his presence. Once inside, the smell of shredded cedar bedding hung in the air that reminded Spencer of the hamster he had as a child, and along one wall there were aquariums and terrariums for a variety of fish and other harmless critters. Cats and birds were in cages on the opposite wall and no doubt tantalized by the sight of all the colorful tropical fish they might like to catch. In the center of the shop there was a high glass walled box with at least six puppies all trying their very best to climb out or be selected.

"Hello," a young lady greeted him. "Looking for anything in particular?"

"Not really. My staff tells me I need a friend in this town and a dog might fit the bill. My problem is I don't spend much time at home and I would hate to have a dog by himself all day. There might be someone else, however, that might need one and will have a lot more time on her hands than me."

"That's very compassionate. I usually hear that a week or two later when they want to bring the dog back. Same with birds, but you never hear about that."

"It would be nice to have dog, but I just can't get attached."

As Spencer talked, a friendly yellow Labrador retriever came up beside him and leaned her head on his leg and held it there.

"I'm Janet and this is Harriet," she said pointing down. "She is the new mom of five adorable pups. Want to see them?"

"Why not, but I hope I don't fall for one."

"I can save you from that," as they walked over to a big box with a side opening and, after lifting up the top, Spencer looked down and saw the pups all huddled and cuddled together. "There're not for sale yet and I think Harriet is a little worried about that. I think she wants to go where they go," she said with a smile.

"I don't think she has anything to worry about with me, but if I could, I would take them all."

"Well, if you change your mind and have the time to take care of one, I hope you will come back. Or have your friend stop in and take a look. It doesn't take much to get attached. Not with these."

"I will. Nice to meet you, Janet. My name is Spencer Tallbridge. Neat name for your store by the way. How did you come up with it?"

"This was the old location for the city dog pound and I didn't think that was such a good name. In a sense, I do sell dogs by the pound though, so it fits."

"Cool" he remarked. "Hope to see you again."

"You will know when you're ready. I'll be seeing you. Goodbye."

Spencer quickly redirected his thinking to the task at hand. He needed two things and he would then be able to get Molly, Mc-Bride and Prescott off his mind. First, he needed Molly's DNA and second, he had to get the swabs from the glove, and he had to do all of this without getting himself fired or prosecuted. He decided that the second necessity was the first place to start.

The next morning Spencer had a full docket with Judge Harris but would have time in the afternoon hopefully to take advantage of Laura Renner being short staffed. After court he assembled and divided his DNA swab kits into two envelops that fit neatly into his front coat pockets. Each one was labeled as the swabs from the same fictitious investigator marked with only a number so that the gender associated with the swabs would not be known to Patterson at the lab. A cigarette from Molly, when he was able to secure it, and also labeled as coming from the Compton crime scene, would complete the operation. The cover story that Spencer would send along with the swabs and cigarette butt would state that the cigarette butt was probably tossed at the scene by an investigator and collected, so it needed to be excluded as somehow involved in the crime and matched the four swabs sent, purportedly to provide good samples for analysis. To Spencer, if they all matched, or closely matched, McBride would positively be confirmed as the killer of Linda Stewart. If there was no match, he had not planned that far ahead and discounted that possibility. In any event, Spencer only considered that the lab would only issue a report and let Spencer deal with it in the Compton case.

Spencer arrived at Central Records and was greeted by a clerk he had not seen before.

"Good afternoon," Spencer said. "Is Laura Renner available? She has worked with me on the review of some old records and I was hoping I would not have to reinvent the wheel, so to speak."

"Sorry," she began. "She cracked a tooth last night and had to go to the dentist. I'm not sure when she will be back, but I'm sure I can help you. Are you an attorney?"

"Yes. I'm with the prosecutor's office. My name is Spencer Tallbridge, an assistant prosecutor. That tooth must really be painful. I appreciate your offer, but I'll just come back in a few days and see how she is doing. If you hear from her, please give her my best."

With that quick ending to a well-planned day, Spencer decided to go to Plan B, the cigarette butt of Molly McBride. He wasn't sure what brand she smoked. He had not bought cigarettes since quitting in college. He did recall that her ashtray was filled and that all the butts had brown filters so one of those brands would have to work. He first thought that he could easily get a butt or two from her ashtray, but there was no positive evidence who had smoked them even though Molly apparently had no friends. Spencer had to be positive and whatever might be apparent would not work for being positive on such an important adventure.

Buying the cigarettes would be the easy part of the plan and there was no plan on how to end up with a clean sample of just Molly's DNA. Telling her the plan could never be an option. If he involved her, it would expose her to everything bad that could happen to him. Besides, her continued confidentiality would always be in serious doubt. He would need to give her the cigarettes, convince her to smoke one and then retrieve it without contaminating it with his own DNA. He thought to himself with a chuckle that using a blue nitrile rubber glove was out of the question. Lastly, he would have to put the cigarette butt into some type of container without letting on what he was up to. However, those were not his worst concerns.

Herald had admonished him to stay away from Molly so he would have to pay her a visit without being noticed. It all started so simply, but now it was becoming more complicated than he ever considered. Imagination was one thing; reality was quite another. He decided to take it one step at a time and see where it went. So far, with Laura Renner, the plan had gone nowhere, and he had to face the prospect that nothing might ever work.

Spencer stopped at what he called a local Stop 'n Rob because it had been held up so many times and checked out the cigarette selection behind the counter.

A clerk politely inquired with a strong Indian accent. "May I help you very much, sir?"

"Yes, I'm looking for filtered cigarettes for a friend. I don't know the brand, but the filters are brown, if that helps."

"Yes. It does help and I think this might do. Does your friend smoke menthol? This one has no menthol."

"I don't think she smokes menthol cigarettes. I'll give that a try."

"That will be $7.42. You can't bring them back, so I hope they are what she wants. Will there be anything else?"

"Thanks for the warning. That's all I need. I can't believe how the price on these has gone up from when I smoked," Spencer said with a smile, paid and left for his apartment.

When he had a chance to assess the situation of how to get Molly's sample, he realized that he would have to become a smoker again for a short time as the only way. He remembered how hard it was to quit and frequently remembered how much he liked, and was dependent upon, cigarettes. After many years now, he hated the smell of it and now he would have to go back to it to share a smoke with Molly. His next concern was how to touch her cigarette butt without contaminating it, and he felt he had a flash of brilliance. No, he could not use a glove, he thought, but he could arrive with bandages on his index finger and thumb injured from hitting both simultaneously with a hammer while hanging a picture. He would just have to put them on when he arrived before knocking. That was the best deception he could come up with and only left the problem of where to put the butt and how to get it out of her ash tray. A plastic bag pocket liner would easily solve the container issue and he would just have to play the acquisition problem by ear or maybe by asking for a glass of water as a distraction and snatch one of her cigarette butts from an ash tray. Either way, by not pressing his luck with more than one visit, he believed he would only have one shot at getting it right.

How to accomplish that without getting caught could be challenging. After Herald's warning which was meant as an order, he became a little paranoid about who was watching him because he never saw anyone he knew while he talked to Molly at the courthouse. He decided that the best way was to park a good distance away, walk to her apartment and take a cue from Prescott by wearing dark glasses and a baseball cap. A hoodie might be better coverage but would more than likely raise suspicions as the disguise of choice by more than some criminals. He finally had it worked out and would put his plan in action the next night.

Chapter Nineteen

As the end of the next day drew closer, Spencer's thoughts turned to the task of getting a sufficient sample of Molly's DNA. As McBride's mother, she would almost be the perfect match for his DNA in the glove, and there would be no other way to make the comparison. Fortunately, he thought, Molly did not use lipstick or makeup of any kind, luxuries she could not afford. Considering her overall mental condition, she had no interest. Spencer had everything ready to go. He fit a plastic Ziplock bag into his right pocket and he put his pack of cigarettes in his shirt pocket where they always used to be. He did not open the pack and would only do that when he was assured Molly would accept the offer to join him. He left his jacket, dark glasses and ball cap in his car as the last remaining items necessary for his performance. Only then did it hit him that smokers have to have a way to light cigarettes. It would not make sense to ask Molly for a light and he did not have one. Hopefully his secretary could help out without having to make a stop for matches or a lighter.

"Amy," Spencer called out, "Where do you keep those matches you used to put on the office birthday candles?"

"Whose birthday? It's not yours, is it?" Amy knew everyone's birthdays in the office.

"Not mine, but I've been here almost six months and I thought I would just put one on a cup cake tomorrow." He surprised himself with how easy it had become to prevaricate. Lies were becoming easy and he took unwelcomed notice of his deception especially with Amy who he had learned to trust. Now he was deceiving her, too, with his confounding plan and briefly wishing that he never got started with it.

"The matches are in the top drawer of the conference room. It's the first drawer on the right and be sure to put them back. No one smokes around here anymore, and I don't want to hunt them down when I need them."

"No problem; Thanks," he said as he walked down to the conference room nearby and retrieved a slightly used pack of matches.

"I'm heading out," Amy announced. "See you tomorrow."

"Me, too. I have a few things to clean up and then I'm outta here," Spencer said, thinking that at the end of the workday Molly would also be heading home from the courthouse so that the best time to approach her was in about an hour. It was now time to put the band aids on his fingers as a last touch.

Spencer was now finally ready to put an essential element of his plan to work. He left the court administrative parking lot and drove randomly around town. He did not think anyone was following, but he had his own sense of guilt that would have made that likely, if anyone knew what he was doing and visiting Molly against the instructions of his boss. He finally parked three blocks away. There was a chill in the air and the sun had set. He felt comfortable that the Prescott hat trick would work without being discovered along with his jacket and dark glasses worn at night. When he arrived at Molly's door, he made one last check that everything was ready at hand and gave the door a firm knocks three times. There was no response and he tried again. After a few minutes and hearing nothing from inside he was about to give it one last try when he heard Molly ask, "Who is it?"

"It's Spencer Tallbridge. Can I talk to you for a minute?"

"I've got nothing more say to you that I have not already said. You know what you are, and you know what that is."

"Really, I don't. I need to ask you something and I can't do it through the door. I really need to talk to you. I think I can help." His offer of help worked before, he thought, and might again. Sure enough, Molly opened the door and, looking disheveled as always, slowly said, "What do you want this time?"

From this point forward Spencer knew it would be unscripted. He did not know what to expect from Molly, and he had to invent a reason to gain her confidence on the fly.

"Mrs. McBride," he began slowly," I want to try something, but I have to be careful. The last guy from our office lost his job trying to help, and I think a cop didn't do too well either." Spencer had no intention of telling her anything about his plan. That plan he would have to take to the grave, if it ever blew up, but he had an idea that was total fiction that just might get her interested enough to sit back, smoke a cigarette with him and listen. It worked.

"OK, I'm listening."

Spencer took the liberty to pull up a kitchen-type chair and took out his pack of cigarettes.

"Let's smoke this over, what do you say?"

"I'd say you're smoking my brand and I'm out. So, I guess the answer is yes," Molly said welcomingly. "What happened to your fingers? Are you a nail biter?" she asked almost exactly as expected and received the scripted response.

"No. I was hanging a picture and hit my finger with a hammer when I was driving the nail," he said as he opened the cigarette pack and tapped out two. He offered one to Molly who immediately rolled the filter on her lips and tongue waiting for a light. At that moment Spencer struck like a viper snatching the cigarette out of her mouth and instantly shouting, "What's that?"

"What's what?" Molly demanded. "What's wrong?"

"Didn't you see it?" Spencer answered. "There was something on the cigarette paper and I don't think you should be smoking it. Here's another," as he smoothly put the snatched cigarette in his waiting pocket lined with the plastic bag and offered her another. The worst was over and now came the hard part as Molly accepted and examined another cigarette from his extended hand and then gave one to himself. He lit hers, then his and did his best not to choke from the experience but could not hold back a sudden cough even though he did not inhale.

"You know, Mrs. McBride, neither one of us should be smoking. I think I'm going to quit. What do you say we both quit?"

"I don't have much in life left, and this," looking at her cigarette, "is about as good as it gets for me."

"I'll tell you what. I am going to quit and I'm leaving these for you."

"You can't buy me off that easy. You know how I feel."

"Mrs. McBride, I wasn't offering you a peace pipe," he said to inject a small amount of serious humor. "I do want you to think about what I want you to do."

"And just what is that?"

"You told me you were with Billy when the crime was committed. Did anyone ever ask you to take a polygraph examination?"

"No. It was never mentioned. No one ever believed me anyway. Not even his lawyers, so it never came up."

"What about when the guys came from the Innocence Project. Did they ever suggest it?"

"No. Is it too late?"

"Mrs. McBride, I really don't know, but I can ask if you want me to."

"What happens if it says I'm lying?"

"Not good, but nothing can be worse for Billy. It could be worth a chance."

Spencer had what he came for, and now he was trying to convince her about something he knew he could never obtain. No one would do it for the defense and surely not Herald. If she did agree, he would only have to let her down later that it could not be done again, adding to her overwhelming guilt and sorrow. Spencer realized too late that he was tampering with a life in a way that he had no business doing and had ground into the quick with no way out except to continue.

"Why don't you think about it for a while and we can talk again, but please this is something that you can never talk about? OK?"

"If you say so, but I'm afraid I might do more harm than good. I mean I told the truth that Billy was with me and that should come out truthful because I believe it to be true, but Herald convinced everyone that I was just mistaken or just lying. So, what good would the test be?"

Spencer appreciated that she had good questions about his phony cover story to get the DNA sample and there was now a way out for him. What concerned him was that he had thrown a straw to Molly to grasp as a last chance for McBride and an affirmative response from Molly was less than immediate. Was she legitimately worried about doing more harm than good or was she lying all the time about the alibi? Spencer decided he was already in too far to quit now or have more than a brief second thought. Besides, he liked the challenge of the plan that had already overtaken his otherwise good and legal judgment.

"Mrs. McBride, I didn't realize how smart you are to put that all together. I suppose you are right and I don't want to make things worse for you, if it won't help your son. I'm really sorry to bother you with this tonight. I hope you understand."

"Your secret is safe with me. I know the last assistant prosecutor got fired because of me, and I don't want that to happen to you, too. I still think you are all murderers. It's not that I hate you. I hate what you are doing and what you stand for when it comes to Billy who is innocent. You should believe that."

Whatever doubts Spencer had about her sincerity evaporated with her concern for him and he felt he could trust her now as far as he could. Painfully, Spencer smoked several more cigarettes with Molly before leaving. He told her that he would continue to think of ways to help but could make no promises. He also told her that Herald warned him to stay clear of her so that Molly would understand why he would not be speaking to her again in the hallways of the courthouse. She understood but added that it would not change what she was saying whenever and wherever she had a chance to berate him. He could not find the courage to tell her he was going to the execution as a witness with Herald scheduled less than a month away and bid her farewell, leaving the remaining pack of cigarettes on her small dinette table as he walked toward her door and left.

Chapter Twenty

When Spencer arrived at his apartment, he felt safe that the first hurdle in his grand plan was a success. The first thing he did was put on two blue nitrile gloves from his briefcase, being careful not to touch anything that might contaminate later results. Only then did he go into his right pocket to remove the Ziplock bag with Molly's cigarette fully intact. Without removing it from the bag, Spencer snapped off its filter and set the bag aside. Then he went back to his case and retrieved the extra glass vial he had and placed it and the plastic bag in front of him at his kitchen counter. Carefully, he removed the filter and placed into the vial and screwed on the top while thinking to himself "mission accomplished". The label was the easy part and he put on an authentic-looking, detective-type label indicating that it was an object from the Compton crime scene and labeled it "Item Number 2" for comparison with the other four from the glove in evidence yet to be obtained that would be numbered one through four later. With the first half of the project completed, he put everything back into his briefcase and settled in for an easy evening of guitar picking and planning the next step. He felt some relief that with all that he had done and said, he had broken no laws. The truth of the lies he had told was known only to him and would hopefully remain so throughout the path he had taken. Hopefully also, he would not experience firsthand those "Five to Ten Blues".

The next morning at his office he called Laura Renner at Central Records. She was back from a painful day at her dentist and was back to her helpful ways.

"Hello, Mrs. Renner. This is Spencer Tallbridge and I was wondering if you might have some time today to help me out again with some evidence again?"

"Of course, and it's Laura, remember? I heard you were in the other day. They asked me who that nice young man was," she said smiling. "Sorry I missed you. I wish I was working instead of where I had to be."

"Right, Laura. I heard you cracked a tooth. Very painful."

"And still is, but not as bad. I have to go back to let the dentist finish a cap that he hopes will work. No guarantees, he said, but I hope I don't have to take more time off. When do you want to come in?"

Spencer realized that if Laura was going to be unavailable sometime in the future with her dental problem, he did not have a lot of time to waste. He sensed that he should move quickly.

"I was thinking this afternoon, if you have time?"

Without saying more, her reply was a simple, "See you here," and hung up.

Spencer had everything he needed ready to go from the first misfire at Central Records. He had everything timed out and just needed five minutes to get it done and get out. "A walk in the park," he thought, and he just needed a little time alone with the glove to finish the second half of his project.

When Spencer arrived at Central Records, Laura Renner seemed to be in an accommodating mood.

"Mr. Tallbridge, glad you could make it. I hear you met my brother Brent."

Spencer was taken aback by her comment and was immediately concerned that he might not be as alone in his adventure as he had hoped.

"Yes. I did. Nice conversation about old times and police work. Glad I bumped into him. Did he tell you much about it?" he asked with the suggestion that their conversation was the result of just a casual and incidental meeting.

"I never thought to ask. It's just funny what a small world it is even after all these years since he left the force. So, what are we looking at again today? More on the Compton case or something else?"

Spencer could not tell one way or another how much she was really told by her brother but took the chance that he kept everything to himself. Spencer decided that it was time to move forward.

"I need to look at the McBride evidence one last time. I made a few notes the last time and misplaced them, so I have to go over it again just to be sure on a couple of points."

"No problem," she said happily and went again to the drawer with the keys to the evidence locker.

"How are you staffed today?" Spencer asked.

"We're in good shape today and should be for a while. You can take all the time you need. I can hang out with you 'til you're done," she said with a smile.

Not exactly what Spencer hoped to hear, but he hoped it might work out as they went to the second floor. She opened the locker with the box of evidence he was after and carefully placed it on the table in the room reserved for examining such contents. Spencer slowly took out each item and kept an eye on the one envelope he was after. He did not set it aside and did not want to call attention to it. His briefcase was at hand and all it would take, he thought, was for Laura to become distracted and he would be home free or so he hoped. Down below on the first floor another voice could be heard, and it was another lawyer looking to review evidence and a transcript from what they both could hear from the reception desk.

"Don't worry," Laura offered. "We have the desk covered so there's no rush. I have all day."

Spencer soon realized that as trusting as Laura was on his first day, she had made a friend that she did not want to part with. Finally, Spencer determined that his plan was not going to work and perhaps he should scrub the whole idea. Certainly his life would be easier. He felt some relief that he would not succeed, but his competitive edge kicked in and he decided to solve the problem with drastic measures. He decided that he would have to break in after hours and take his chances and he didn't know what those would be.

"I think I have found everything I need to know," as he fumbled through a number of exhibits that were meaningless to him except the one he was after and the one he would leave on top of all the rest. "Sure glad you have a secure facility here. I didn't see any kind of security system though."

"You mean like those eyes in the ceiling like at the shopping malls?" she asked. Answering her own question, she volunteered, "We're lucky the crooks don't know we're here. Just old locks on the doors and that's about it."

"About it?" Spencer asked. "Nothing more?" Spencer asked incredulously.

"No, that's it, but we've never had a break in. Can't think of anything anyone would want to steal. Can you?"

"No. Sure can't," as they headed back down to the first floor and he said goodbye to Laura. As he left, he took one last look around and saw a side entrance in an alleyway next to another building that looked unoccupied. This is where plan B would have to start, he thought, wishing that he had simply pocketed the evidence in the first place even though there was never such an opportunity that he considered at the time of their first meeting.

When Spencer got in his car, he went to start the engine, but stopped and sat back to think over what he had just decided must be done. Now he was about to go from liar to felon with a breaking and entering charge, and the things he was doing were starting to pile up. To this point, he again considered that he had not committed any crimes and if his plan was to succeed, he would have to break into Central Records and he did not know the first thing about how to do that other than what he had learned about criminal conduct in court. Usually, that was accomplished with a swift kick to a door or a broken window and neither of those were viable options. Like in the movies, he thought, he would have to pick the lock to the side door in the dark and how to do that was a mystery with the need for instruction. Talking to a cop might be the best place to start and he drove off to Alibis in the hope of enlisting some help.

"Hey Jake," Spencer called out to a familiar face as he entered the bar. Finnegan was faithfully manning his post behind the bar, and Jake was having a beer with a couple of other patrol officers Spencer had not met.

"Come on over," Jake replied. "I hear you met Petty Petty and Duffy a while back. I want you to meet a couple of other badges."

"I just met Petty and Duffy. I didn't know Petty had a brother on the force."

"He doesn't. Petty was a Chief Petty Officer in the Navy. So we call him Petty Petty just to get under his skin," he said with a laugh. "How's it going?"

"Well enough, but I've got a problem. I brought a locker with me when I moved and I lost the key. I'm trying to figure out how to open the lock without breaking everything."

One of the two officers with Jake introduced himself and the other and asked if it was a padlock and that a problem like that would best be solved with a bolt cutter or hack saw. Spencer said it was a lock like on an old door. The other patrol officer joined in and said that his experience was with Slim Jims and Lock Jocks that were devices for opening car doors and that lock picks were more in Jake's background as a detective.

"I think I know what you need," Jake said, "and I think I can help you out. You need a bump key. Works every time."

"What the hell is a bump key?" Spencer asked. "Is it like a lock pick you see in the movies?"

"Nope. It's just a special key. Real easy to make and criminals make them all the time. Unlike a lock pick you see in movies, a bump key is quick and easy. Not so easy with real lock picks. At least, that's what the burglars tell me."

"Will it work on old locks?" Spencer asked, considering the age of the doors at Central Records.

"The older the better," Jake said, "and here's how it works," as he took out a ring of keys from his pocket. "The key looks just like my door key here except all the peaks and valleys are the same. Now that alone won't open your locker, but if you put that special key in, put a little turning pressure on it and give it a bump, the key will magically turn and open."

"What's the magic? Do you know?" Spencer asked.

"There is a tiny spring-loaded rod that fits on the top of each peak of the key when you put it in. When the key is bumped in, get it, bumped in, the little rods jump up and then down, but your turning pressure causes them all to hang up on the edge of the cylinder that allows the key to continue to turn and thus open the lock. Pretty cool, right? You can Google 'bump key' and get a better description, but I think you get the picture."

"I do and that's about as cool as anything I've heard of in a long time. That could be really handy for a guy like me that loses keys. Where can I get one? Is it legal to buy one?"

"Believe it or not you can order one on the net, but don't bother. I'll drop off my set in the morning. I got it years ago in a burglary case, and we keep it handy for just such problems. There will be more than one key so you just have to fit one that will slide into your lock and the rest is easy. Just give it a bump with a light hammer. And I do mean a light bump. I'll do it for you if you have any problems. Otherwise just get the set back to me when you're finished."

The offer was not lost on Spencer as he considered what Jake would say if he only knew the truth. For now, the truth had taken a back seat and hopefully would never have to be disclosed. "Great. I'll see you at the office around ten if that works and I'm sure I can figure it out. Thanks for the offer."

"See you at ten," Jake concluded.

Spencer stayed on for a respectable amount of time and talked the small talk of law and order as only police and prosecutors could do in the best place in town before heading home to consider his next night out to break into Central Records. The bump key would have to come first.

Chapter Twenty-One

As Spencer was driving home, still satisfied that progress had been made on his grand plan, he once again reverted to thoughts about how far into the weeds he had gotten with the lies and fictions he created. He had indeed ground into the quick as his father warned, and the reality of what he was about to do and what he might lose started to sink in deeper than ever before. Suddenly a blast from a horn behind caused him to realize that the deeper he was in thought the slower he drove, which caused him to start paying attention to his driving and not the future of his career and his chosen profession. Thinking too much and driving was always a problem for Spencer, who knew that he could drive and chew gum at the same time but thinking and driving was always a problem. It was time now to give his father one last call before implementing what he knew in his heart he had to do.

When Spencer arrived at his apartment, he had no appetite for dinner. Calling his father became a principal concern. Five minutes on high in the microwave, his usual recipe for his dinner, would have to wait, he thought, and placed the call.

"Hello, Dad," he began as usual.

"Hello, Son," his father responded also as usual. "How's it going out there?"

"I know you have a lot invested in me and I might be screwing it up."

"You're not in jail, are you?" his father said laughing. "You need me to go your bond?"

Spencer hesitated just long enough for his father to understand the seriousness of the call.

"Not yet, but maybe. I may have ground into the quick this time with a harebrained idea that might end badly and embarrass the hell out of you."

"What is it, Son? What's going on?" his father asked with no humor in his voice.

"It's along the idea of what I told you earlier when you said to follow my conscience. Well I have and I will probably break the law before it's over and lose everything. And I mean everything."

"Is it worth it?" his father asked without first asking for details or an explanation.

"I've been telling myself that it is, but I haven't had to pay the price yet. I'm getting close to that and I'm having second thoughts."

"Other than your license and maybe jail, what's at stake?"

"I can quit now. I can turn my back and never look back. A murderer will die and it will bother me for the rest of my life and I will never know if I was right or if I was wrong.

"Why do you care about a murderer?"

"I don't really, but there is a part of me in this whole deal that keeps telling me I have to look at it. I have to find out. I have to confirm that this guy deserves to die and I think I can do it. There was another assistant prosecutor like me five years ago that apparently thought the same thing or got sucked in the same way I am and ended up getting fired. That won't be the worst of it for me because I have a better plan. It just happens to be illegal as hell."

"If I taught you right, you're between that old rock and the hard place."

"You taught me right, Dad."

"If you believe that, here's what I think. If you know what is right and are willing to pay the consequences to prove it, do it. You get in trouble, I've always said, when you weigh in on personal consequences to compromise your conscience. If things go sour, I could use a handout here and you know your stuff. I know I taught you right and sometimes doing the right thing is not always black or white and in one of your law books. Racehorses again for me might be a good change of pace anyway."

"I needed that. I'll do my best not to screw this up."

"I know, Son. Can you tell me what you are about to do and when?"

"No. I think it best, if I don't. Probably the less you know the better. If this blows up, I don't want you involved."

"I'll try to stay optimistic."

"I remember what you said about optimism once when we were knee deep in horse shit. 'With all the horse shit, there must be a pony around here somewhere,'" he said injecting a little humor to the country wisdom his father gave him. "I'm hoping to find a pony, but so far I'm knee deep. One way or another, I'll let you know. Great to talk to you. I'll keep in touch.

"Bye, Son. Good luck."

###

The next morning Spencer arrived early at his office. His mind was firmly made up to finish what he started. He considered using his office computer to look into bump keys because he did not have a computer set up at his new apartment. It occurred to him, however, that a check of his computer might lead to evidence against him, so he just waited for Jake to stop by. Thinking like a criminal was foreign to him, and it was hard to rationalize that he was on the right side of whatever argument he might conceive to justify what he was doing.

"Detective Jake Butler is here to see you," Amy called out. "Do you want me to bring him back?" she asked.

"Yes. Please," Spencer replied.

A few minutes later Butler was brought into his office with his Visitor Pass in place.

"This place is getting to be like Fort Knox. Do you think anyone out there or in here doesn't know me?" he asked scornfully.

"Don't take it personally. With McBride's execution coming up, Herald isn't taking any chances. He says the last thing he needs is something getting in the way of a good news story, if you know what I mean. He wants the focus on the execution and not on him until it's over and he says finally over."

"I've seen it all before. Well, here's your bump key set," as he tossed a ring of keys to Spencer.

Spencer thanked him and looked over each key and then began to ask questions

"They all seem to look alike"

"Not really. Look closer. They all have a little different length and they work for all the older-style door keys. Newer ones can't be bumped as easy, but if you have an older lock, one of these will fit."

"Each one has this little rubber thing at the base of the key. What's that for? Should I take them off when I try to put one in the keyhole?"

"That's a rubber O-ring and it helps with the bump. It's sort of like a bumper. Push the key all the way to the O-ring and the hold the key in your left hand and put some turning pressure on it to the right, just like turning a key. It won't turn, but the pressure is needed. Next, while holding the pressure, give the key a tap straight in with a hammer. Not too much and when you do, the key should turn to unlock. Got it?"

"Got it. I didn't think it was so easy to be a burglar. How did you catch the guy with these?"

"He was smart as far as keys were concerned, but he used a flashlight without a filter and we saw the light."

"What filter?" Spencer asked with muted amazement and special interest.

"It's a red filter over the end of a flashlight. It's just a piece of clear red plastic wrapper, anything clear and red will do. And you use a rubber band to hold it in place. Light through a red filter is almost impossible to see at a distance and it doesn't mess up night vision, but regular light is easy to see and does affect night vision when the white light is turned off. That's what gave him away."

"Interesting. Never would have thought of that."

"You can use it in your next burglary," Butler said prophetically without having any idea of what Spencer had in mind. The irony was not lost on Spencer who grimaced at the thought.

"Thanks. I will. By the way I sent the board up to the lab and I hope to get a favorable report to make our lives easy."

"If you say so. I expect the defense to come up with some excuse even if the defendant's DNA is all over it."

"We'll see, but I hope not," Spencer responded.

From Spencer's conversation with Detective Butler, he realized he had more work to do. He had not thought through the lighting situation concerning the alley to the side door of Central Records or what light would be available once he got in to avoid being caught by the likes of Butler. It would be dark in a couple of hours after work and he would need a good flashlight with a red filter and he had neither. After work his first stop was a hard-ware store to pick up a flashlight and look for some material to use as a filter. Pete and Paula's Hardware was on his way home, so he stopped in to see what they had. It was a store that had a little bit of everything, and everything was stacked to the ceiling. Their motto was "If they make it, we can get it" and service was the order of the day in their store. They compete with the big box operators that were putting the mom and pops out of business, so what they had to sell was service, even if the prices were a lit-tle higher, just to stay in business.

"Can I help you, sir?" a clerk asked eagerly as Spencer barely made it in the door.

"I'm just looking for a small flashlight and some clear red cellophane."

"You a pilot?" the clerk asked trying to show his hard-ware-sense of knowledge toward problem solving.

"No. What makes you thinks so?"

"Well it's the red plastic and flashlight. Maybe a bad as-sumption, but pilots use flashlights with red filters because of night vision problems caused by regular light, so I thought that was what this was about. Sorry. Same thing with the dark rooms of photographers, but they don't do much of that anymore. It's all digital," he said offering more information than Spencer ex-pected or wanted.

"No need to be sorry. I actually need it to do some work in the dark and need to make a red filter for the flashlight," Spencer cautiously explained without letting on that he was considering something criminal.

"This is easy. I have just the thing. A small light that uses two triple-A batteries. It comes with three filters and the best one is red in my opinion. There's an instruction on how to open the light part to place the filter. Very simple."

"That's what I need. I'll take it. How long do the batteries last?"

"I'm guessing two hours non-stop and batteries come with it. I'm not trying to sell batteries, but you never know about the ones that come with these packages. I would buy a couple more just to play it safe if you're concerned about running out of light."

"I need to play it safe, nothing dangerous, but I'd hate to be caught in the dark after going to all this trouble."

"I completely understand," the clerk responded, and Spencer felt safe that the clerk had no idea of what was to come and, for that matter, neither did he.

Spencer had one last request and he decided to keep his string of deceptions going. There was a moment of regret that he was getting used to it and doing it well.

"I'm hanging a couple of pictures and I need a small light hammer to put in a few tacks. I don't need a big carpenter's hammer. Just a small one will do. Do you have one of those?"

"Sure do and it is called a tack hammer. I think this is just what you need," as he reached for a small tack hammer hanging on a wall with several other types.

"This will work just fine," Spencer said, paid and left the store with everything he needed.

After leaving the hardware store, it was past sundown and was almost dark. The weather was cool and clear with no adverse weather expected until the weekend. He decided to drive by Central Records just to see what he called the lay of the land. For Spencer, it would be like a military operation without the necessary experience to make it work. Just the same he knew instinctively that working in the dark with a red-filtered flashlight and being caught breaking in by the police on routine patrol would be a career ending problem. Spencer checked the time, found a place to park and pretended to be reading a few documents while watching the traffic in the area out of the corner of his eye. To his surprise, after an hour and a half, he never saw a cruiser or foot traffic and only light auto traffic. He decided that the next night at the same time would be the night to finally put his plan in action.

Chapter Twenty-Two

During work the next day Spencer was totally distracted. He had a plan, but no plan if he was caught. He thought about how he would explain himself to his father and Herald and those thoughts were constantly playing without an answer. The easy way out was to quit. As the reality of what he planned to do sunk in deeper than ever before, he again considered that quitting was his best option as he made his way to another court appearance in the courtroom of Judge Harris. As expected, the reality of Molly was also there, and she was faithfully manning her self-imposed post of duty to give Spencer his daily dose of hell.

"Back again, murderer?" Molly shouted sneeringly as he walked by.

"Why not," he responded with a tone of exasperation. "I don't suppose I could at least get you to quit smoking," he said sarcastically while looking around to make sure no one else heard him. Molly made no reply as he hastily entered the court-room already in session.

"Nice of you to join us, Mr. Tallbridge," the Judge said from his bench with a mix of questionable and sarcastic appreciation.

"Sorry I'm late, Judge. It's been one of those days when everything piles up. It won't happen again. I promise," he said apologetically.

"Don't make promises you can't keep, especially those you make to yourself," the Judge admonished with the force of judicial authority in his voice.

Those words were enough for Spencer to get a hold of himself. He was sure of himself the day and the weeks before. This was no time to break his promise to himself. So, he took the Judge's words to heart as a calm settled over his distraction. The plan was on, and he would have to see it to the end regardless of the chastisement he would again receive from Molly and her hate-filled words as he left the courtroom.

After work, it was another night with dinner out of the question. He had no appetite. Once back at his apartment, he assembled all the implements necessary for his mission. He had a list that included a ball cap, jacket, rubber gloves, and flashlight with red filter, extra batteries, bump key set, hammer, eyewash and two envelopes each with two vials and two Q-tips which were extra-long to easily reach down into each finger of the glove. He would take nothing more and leave nothing behind including his own fingerprints, if he could pull it off. Like Santa, he checked his list twice to make sure he did not miss anything. Unlike Santa, there was no chimney to magically drop into Central Records and breaking in through its side door was now two hours away. After carefully assembling everything he needed, he put on his jacket, ball cap and sat back in his chair waiting for daylight to end and his adventure or misadventure in the unknown to begin.

Chapter Twenty-Three

As forecast, it was another cool and clear evening in September as Spencer left the safety of his apartment. He looked back as he drove out of his parking lot and wondered if he would see it the same way when, or if, he returned. All things having been considered over and over, he resolved finally that there was no turning back, but said out loud to himself as his only audience,

"What the hell am I doing?"

When he was a few blocks away from Central Records, he decided to park there to avoid anyone associating him with his car and to give him a few blocks to see if anyone else was walking in the area. As he approached Central Records, he saw that the coast was clear and the inside of the building was in total darkness. As he passed the alley and saw no one, he made a military right face and hurried to the side door with the bump key set in hand. He started with the first key on the ring into the keyhole and it would not go in. Then a second with the same result. Hoping that three was a charm, he was rewarded with an easy insertion all the way to the rubber bumper. With his left hand he put right turning pressure on the key as Butler instructed and reached to his belt that held his tack hammer like a gun holster. With it he gave the end of the key a light tap, and as advertised, the key turned and unlocked the door. He quickly entered and stepped into the darkness of the building, feeling safe and secure that his first crime had not been discovered. But this was not, he thought, a time to reassess on every rule of life and his profession he had violated. The means had to justify the ends, he also thought, and would not bode well for him in a court of law, if this is where all this was headed.

Once inside, he took out a pair of the rubber gloves he brought along to avoid contamination of the evidence he sought and to avoid detection if anyone started a burglary investigation. Fortunately, he brought extras because the first one he put on ripped at the fingers and he carefully put it in his empty back pocket. He was more careful with the next one realizing that he could not make many of those kinds of mistakes. Next he took out his flashlight with the red filter and it worked perfectly to give him just enough light to avoid stumbling over chairs or running into cabinets as he walked over to Laura Renner's desk to get her cabinet keys. Fortunately, her desk was not locked and the keys were still in her top right drawer tied to a six-inch wooden stick. He took the keys and left the drawer open to return them when he finished.

He then made his way to the second floor. In near darkness, except the small area lit by his flashlight, everything looked different. He had not anticipated that problem, but he was still able to get his bearings by looking at the surroundings. He knew the cabinet he was after was about in the middle and he was able to calculate the one he needed by a doorway to the reviewing room behind him. His calculation worked out as he was able to quickly unlock the cabinet that held the box of evidence from the McBride case he was after.

Carefully and quietly he removed the evidence box and placed it on the table of the reviewing room. He had turned off his flashlight and saw that there was some light from outside coming through a window of the room and that he might throw a shadow. There was a shade that could easily have been thirty years old and may not have been used in years, and he carefully and slowly pulled it down, hoping that no one on the outside would notice. The shade still worked and now he was once again in total darkness which he lit up just enough with his flashlight to accomplish his mission.

The envelope containing the rubber glove was where he left it the last time he was there, eliminating a minor concern that someone might have been on to him. Before opening the envelope, he took out his supplies from the pockets of his jacket. He put the vials in front of him and next the bottle of eyewash that he opened and kept within arm's reach. The Q-tips were in each kit with the vials and he would take them out one at a time as he swabbed the four fingers. It was now time to take the samples. Spencer laid his flashlight on the table pointing it in the general direction of the tasks at hand. There was just enough light to work with. He carefully removed the evidence glove and held it in his left hand. He then took a Q-tip from the first vial and dipped it into the eyewash. Once saturated, he carefully extended the tip down into the inside of the thumb of the evidence glove and twisted it around to swab its entire inner surface. Once accomplished, he put the entire Q-tip into the vial and sealed it with the cap. "One down and three to go," he thought. He had already made the decision not to test one finger and leave it in the condition he found it, in case there ever was any question of what the results were. He decided that the little finger would be elected and selected for that purpose. He was amazed at how calm he was. He had gotten this far without his heart pumping out of his chest or the adrenaline rush he anticipated. It seemed as though it was just business as usual, and soon he would be on his way with the worst over or so he hoped.

The next finger, the middle finger, was just as easy and completed with assembly- line efficiency. As he tightened the vial cap, he heard a noise from below and then the interior first floor lights went on. Now his heart was pumping out of his chest, and he had the adrenaline rush he had earlier anticipated. He froze in place and turned off his flashlight which accomplished little to keep him from being discovered. He waited for footsteps coming up the stairs and thought about what he would say. "Hello," he thought, as an answer to, "What are you doing here?" "I just stopped by to burglarize your evidence locker and get myself prosecuted." There was no humor in his thoughts. Only resignation to an inescapable situation of his own making. He waited and heard nothing more. Minutes passed and still nothing. By now his hands were shaking almost uncontrollably and he knew that he would have a difficult time even to talk, if questioned about his presence. Still there was no sound except the gushing of blood through his inner ears and at that moment the lights went off. There was a faint sound of a door closing and he was once again in near total darkness, shaken, but undiscovered.

Spencer considered wrapping up his plan. He had enough samples, he thought, and his hands continued to shake involuntarily. He was not sure he could even put the Q-tip into the eye awash without spilling it. He made a lousy burglar, he thought to himself. Leaving the last sample behind was perhaps the best option considering his circumstances, but if he played it out that way, he knew that he would always wonder if that last sample would have made a difference, so he pressed on. He needed a moment to collect his thoughts and calm down and the moment turned into what seemed to be the eternity of minutes with a calming result. He was now back to the business at hand. Now, he thought, was not the time to spill the eyewash, and he was able to dip the last Q-tip into it without difficulty. Calmly, he thought, "Even if it does spill, there won't be any residue. The evidence will completely evaporate." He amazed himself that he could think so scientifically under the circumstances and once again he was thinking like a burglar, he thought, along with all the personal disgust that went with being one. He carefully and deliberately used a Q-tip saturated with eyewash to successfully sample the last remaining finger of the rubber glove. Carefully, he put all four vials in his coat pocket along with the eyewash and repackaged the evidence glove that he returned to the box of other evidence. He then methodically returned the evidence box to the cabinet, locked it and checked to see that he had everything he came in with and double checked that he had left nothing behind. Burglars, he thought, leave nothing behind unless they do so on purpose, and he had no plan to do that. It gave him a moment's pause to wonder why the rubber glove was left behind in the first place. No doubt McBride was no professional.

Spencer kept his gloves on as he took the cabinet key stick back to Laura Renner's desk. As he pointed his red light at the drawer, he was instantly startled to see that the drawer he had left open for the later return of the key was now closed. It had to be the person who came in, he thought, but he wasted no time deliberating the why of that for now and put the key back in the drawer. Then, finally, he made his way to the exit where he had entered a half hour earlier, looked through the door window as best he could that no one was in the vicinity, opened the door and left leaving the door to lock behind him. Once he was out, he put his flashlight in his hip pocket along with his gloves that he quickly stripped off and with every step he took out of the alley he felt the safety of anonymity returning.

When he reached the street, however, he saw that he was not as alone as he had hoped. Some distance away at a dimly lit street corner he saw the dark figure of a person. He could not tell if it was a man or woman, someone young or old. It was just a person who was looking in his direction and not moving or saying anything. Spencer looked momentarily the other way to cross the street to put more distance between them and when he looked back the person was gone. He questioned if he just imagined the phantom resulting from the enormous pressure he had just been under.

By the time Spencer got back to his apartment, many thoughts swirled around inside his head about what he had just done. Yes, he got away clean, he thought. No one might ever have to know. He might not even submit the samples as planned, but he knew that he had committed a crime. Perhaps it was only a trespass and not as severe as a burglary, he rationalized correctly, but he felt little comfort in that legal technical understanding. Either way, he thought, he was now facing the possibility of being caught and fired for his criminal entry, prosecuted and disbarred. These were all known to him going in, but now they all seemed so much more real. He now had a good sense from this true-life experience of what it means to have reality setting in. If he were caught somehow through the testing process, his resulting confession and the reasons for his actions would probably lead to another delay in McBride's execution and the only ones that would benefit again would be Molly and her son. As his mind started to fracture on thoughts of his own destruction, he wondered if Molly planned this all along. He just as quickly dismissed those thoughts as the product of an overwhelming guilt and desire to blame Molly for his own unassisted invention. And then there was the ever-present question of who came to Central Records and for what purpose.

Spencer was certain that he left the key drawer open and that it was closed when he returned the key. If it was Renner, he thought, she would have seen that the drawer was open and the key was missing. She would have even called the police, suspecting that a burglary was in progress and she would not dare go to the second floor to check on her beloved files and evidence. Perhaps, if it was Renner, she simply thought that some other clerk somehow misplaced it, closed the drawer and left. Perhaps she had come back for something left behind, closed the drawer without noticing the absence of the key and left the building without any further concern. Or was it her brother coming to check on him? But that was more inconceivable than any other explanation and nothing was gained, he thought, by trying to know the unknowable and it was best to just talk himself into believing that nothing bad happened at all to him, so far. Tomorrow, he thought, would be another day and he could worry about it then, if the need arose. For the time being, he believed, he had ground into the quick and did not get kicked in the head.

###

The next day Spencer took the vials with the swabs and marked each one as coming from the same donor and labeled them Investigator Number One. He had already marked the vial containing Molly's cigarette filter as coming from the scene in the Compton case for comparison with the samples of Investigator Number One. Patterson already had the board and Compton's DNA sample and he should have been working on them. Spencer called Patterson at the state lab to let him know that the additional evidence he needed to be examined was on its way and that an office investigator would hand deliver the samples that day. He wanted to reaffirm with Patterson that all he needed was a comparison of the board DNA, if any, and Compton's DNA and to exclude the cigarette filter as coming from the fictitious investigator on the other four vials to keep it simple. He also hoped to get the results as soon as possible because the McBride execution was just weeks away. Spencer was less concerned with that schedule because of his overall belief that McBride was guilty and nothing would change that regardless of when the results were obtained. The Compton case was also coming up fast, so an overall fast turnaround of the results would be appreciated.

"Hello, Agent Patterson. It's your student, Spencer Tallbridge, and those samples are on their way today for analysis. I'm having them hand delivered."

"Hi, Spencer. Tell me again about what you need? I remember you wanted tests expedited. Hope I can do that. We're really jammed up here with rape kits."

"You already have a board in a case that was never examined for DNA and compared with the perp's DNA sample that you have on file. He's been in prison for five years. We talked about this case earlier. There are a few other swabs that I told you were also coming. There was an investigator on scene and he may have tossed a cigarette butt while he was there and I expect he did do just that. I need to include him or exclude him as related to the cigarette butt. The perp never smoked, so we know it's not from him, and it would be OK if it were from the investigator."

"I do have the board along with Compton's DNA, as I recall, and it's on my list. If the butt is not from the investigator, then what?" Patterson asked.

"Then it means nothing and it's just a cigarette butt that could be anyone's. So, if there is no match, then no big deal. I just have to say I had it tested for comparison. Make it easy on yourself and don't do anything more, if you don't mind, because I am just trying to include the investigator or exclude him. Would you mind issuing a separate report dealing with the cigarette filter instead of putting it all together in one report? I think it will make it easier for the defense attorney to understand what I will be explaining to him."

"Sure. I can do that. Usually we put everything on one submission sheet, but I understand what you're doing," Patterson said.

"I know you're jammed, but do you think you can get this out quick. The perp's case is coming up quick and I would like to jam up that guy, too," Spencer said with a laugh.

"I'll do my best. It's an old case. I'll start on it when I get your stuff. So long."

"So long and thanks."

Spencer had acted as professionally as any assistant prosecutor and as crooked as any liar. His narrative was one big lie except for the Compton evidence. That did not diminish for an instant the deception practiced by Spencer in his call to his professional friend. Lying had become easy for Spencer as it was with the criminals he formerly represented. And now he knew firsthand how easy it was, how creative he could be and how far he had strayed from the teachings of honesty his father had instilled in him years ago. Until now, he had lived by those teachings and now he had forsaken them for the purpose he also believed was honorable, humane and necessary to do as a member of the human race.

Chapter Twenty-Four

On the eve of McBride's execution, Spencer did not sleep well. He was in and out of consciousness, that in-between place where there is no rest – just killing time. He considered taking an over-the-counter sleep aid that usually worked when he was all hyped up before a trial, but he didn't want to take a chance that he would oversleep and miss picking up Herald. As the night wore on, he tried to think of anything but the execution. The death of McBride was not the problem. He always expected that. He had made a connection with Molly and, so far, he had failed her. "Why should I care?" he repeated to himself over and over with never an answer that would let him sleep. With the execution now only hours away, his failure was complete. He never received the call from Patterson with the analytical results. He knew the results would not make a difference, but with them, he could have lessened Molly's burden of guilt before the execution that had always been his grand plan. He blamed only himself for not pressing Patterson harder than he had, and his rationalization that 'a watched pot never boils' was not working for him now.

Eventually, he thought, he would get the results after the execution and there would be time to explain it all to Molly. There was a fleeting moment of comfort with this, but then came the assumption that Molly would be willing to listen or even be there. Suddenly, on that last thought, and for the first time, he was forced to consider how Molly might respond to her son's death with her certainty of his innocence. It was a thought he had to repel, if he was going to get through the day. It was a day coming that he would just have to ride out to the end. He had hoped that the scheduled trial of the Compton case would be his excuse for not playing chauffeur for Herald, but the delay in the DNA analysis also forced a continuance of that case.

At 5:30 A.M. his cell phone rang; it was Arnold calling. There was a brief moment of hope that another delay had been granted and the trip was off. It was not to be. Arnold was just calling to make sure he was awake and would meet Herald at the office parking lot for the two-hour trip to Lucasville, where the Southern Ohio Correctional Facility is located nearby in Scioto County. There was a construction problem with the interstate that would have made an easier trip to the facility, and so county roads would predominate. An early start was required. The execution was scheduled for 10:30 A.M. and the Attorney General was slated to be in attendance and possibly the Governor who championed the causes of abused and battered women for his election. The Governor hoped those optics would drown out the expected cry of the anti-death penalty protesters who were always on call for the death vigil and post-execution commentary. They wouldn't leave until the McBride hearse was photographed leaving the institution.

"Hello, Mr. Arnold. Still a go?" Spencer asked.

"Yep, just checking to make sure you're on the move. I'd hate it if you screwed this up for the boss. Give me a call when you get back and give me a full report. I've been at a few of these, and I would like to know if anything has changed from the last time. You know, like seating and location of witnesses. The press will be all over this so I might see you on TV. Take my advice and let Herald do all the talking."

"No problem there. He's the master at that stuff and I expect a lesson. I'll give you a call when we get back."

Spencer did not waste any time getting a shower to clear his head and turning on his prefilled coffee pot. He had laid out what he considered his trial suit, a clean white shirt and red tie. He wanted to at least look the part of an assistant prosecutor even if his heart was only half in. By 6:30 A.M. he was on his way. As Spencer pulled into the parking lot, he saw Herald's car and Herald apparently saw him too and got out with his briefcase.

"Morning, Tallbridge. Beautiful day for the needle," he said expecting a laugh from his execution humor as he got in the car.

"Yes, sir. Can't wait," Spencer said with a neutral dead pan response to the callousness of the question.

"I know it's your first time and I can understand the humanity of it all for the uninitiated, but you'll get used to it. I know it's a go, in case you are wondering if there will be another last-second delay. I got a call late yesterday from the Attorney General who filled me in on the last-minute maneuvers by Mc-

Bride's defense team. They put it out that McBride would admit everything in exchange for life without parole and the offer was turned down flat. That should put an end to the 'what if's'. There really is nothing left now except to get this over with. I really hate the drive over to Lucasville. Nothing but back roads and I'm a little tired so I really appreciate you doing the driving today. I'll probably let someone else do it next time."

"Thanks. I really don't mind and I feel it's something I should experience firsthand. Not the drive; I mean the execution. I'm sure it won't be the last execution for our office, and I need to know what to expect even if I don't try those cases. I see you brought your briefcase and, if you don't mind me asking, what's in it?"

"Lesson Number One. The press will tackle us when this is over and we might be surrounded by protesters. That's when I will pull out my copies of the bloody photos and hold them up in both hands telling the world on TV and in the press that I stand for the victim and that McBride got what he deserved."

"Never thought of that."

"Years of experience. You're young. You'll learn."

"Seems like a much better way of explaining things than going intellectual."

"Intellectual! Hell with that. You never get anywhere with those people with a thoughtful argument for the death penalty. You need to hit them right between the eyes or kick their ass with photos of the victim. That usually shuts them up. You have to take a strong stand or get your own ass kicked."

"I agree. I was just wondering how you handle the 'what if's' that an innocent person might be executed?"

"OK. How do you answer that?"

Spencer quickly realized that he better start thinking like Herald since his test for Herald had been turned into a test for him. With only a short pause to collect his thoughts, he began.

"I'd say that there never has been an innocent person in modern times that had been wrongly executed and that the length of time it takes to execute someone insures that result even as we complain about it."

"Perfect answer. I think you get it. I like the delay part. I hadn't really thought about that and since delays are a court problem and not mine, we can still get credit for complaining about it knowing all the while there is nothing we can do about it. You never had a death penalty case when you were on the other side as I recall."

"No. We had complex cases in the public defender's office while I was there, but never a death penalty case. Everyone was always hoping for the chance, the challenge and all, but it never happened for us. I heard all the arguments for and against it, and the one that seemed to make the most sense against it was that anyone over sixty-five at the time of the crime could never be executed. The condemned would die of natural causes before an execution could take place."

"It is hard to disagree with that. So, you're making an equal protection argument? That's been done before and got no traction. As a practical matter, 25% of all condemned die of natural causes anyway."

Spencer could not make the connection between the practical matter and the equal protection argument, but he thought it best not to challenge Herald on his intellectual process. He had already heard Salyers opine on the same arguments and realized where he heard them first.

Herald continued. "Fortunately, we live in a state where it is still available. Some of the worst crimes I have ever seen take place in states where execution is no longer an option. Not much deterrent there and look what they get. Some miserable low life, who has no humanity, deserves none and gets a break. Well, not here. Like I always say, we deter these sons-of-bitches one needle at a time."

"I get the point," Spencer said trying to inject a little humor in the conversation. "But do you think anyone really cares the next day or the next week?" he asked.

"I think so," Herald replied, "as we keep adding to the numbers and continue to normalize the process. That's what it is after all. It's numbers and process, and we do it better than anywhere in the world."

Spencer fought back the counterpoint that the United States is among the few countries that still have the death penalty and that those other countries that still have the process are only out done by the modernization of U.S. methods only in the last minutes of life of the condemned. All still share the torture of time waiting and thinking about the last day of life to come and not be considered cruel or unusual by any standard. It was just a part of the necessary process. All the same, Spencer still held to the principle that the law is there to follow and he took an oath to follow it. The rest is just arguments on morality and the reality of Spencer's place in history even if Herald's logic was flawed. Still, Spencer decided to press further.

"What concerns me the most is the number of DNA exonerations for those on death row. It just seems that the odds are that eventually the exoneration will be a day late and a dollar short, as they say," Spencer noted.

"Not my problem. I don't do odds. I do facts and the facts follow the law. Do your case right and you won't have a DNA problem. Do your case right and you won't have a problem with me either. If the system fails somewhere else, it's not our problem. Do you get that point?"

"Yes, I do and I remember the day I was hired Arnold telling me that we don't do crap shoots," Spencer said, "and I believe getting the death penalty in other counties is a crap shoot. There, it's just the luck of the twelve jurors you draw once guilt is established. Your record in that game, however, is simply outstanding. You're the T. Rex of convictions and the death penalty, and I'm just wondering how you have been so successful when others with the same type of cases end up with life without parole?"

"Are you thinking that what I do is somehow not fair?" Herald asked.

"Not at all," Spencer quickly responded. "It's just that your success plays into the claim that there is an unfair or unequal application that just depends on the skill of the prosecutor."

"Or lack of it, right? That's what is really missed," Herald continued. "Somehow I think you're giving me a backhanded compliment. We don't have the best in other counties going after it or defending against it. I would never tell them that but look at what you usually get. Politicians. Administrators. Bureaucrats on the state side. And the public defenders are no better. No offense."

"None taken. I know there was not that much out there when I applied," Spencer acknowledged, "and I have done my best to prove that a former court-appointed defense lawyer has the right stuff to do this job."

"You have acquitted yourself well, so I really am not putting you in that category," Herald explained. "But to be honest, you could have been, if you didn't do such a good job. The one thing that has always bothered me, however, is that it only takes one juror to vote against the death penalty, a hung jury on the issue, to result in life without. The legislature voted to keep the death penalty by a simple majority, but an eleven-to-one vote by a jury for death and it's life without automatically. That just doesn't seem right to me or make sense."

"Interesting point that I never heard of before. Have you ever put that out to the politicians?"

"Once and it went nowhere. I don't think he got the point and I mean 'he'. I have never had much luck with women politicos on the issue, but they always seem to look for my endorsement around election time even with my record. Are you slowing down?"

"Sorry. I do that when I get too deep into conversations like this when I'm driving. I'll pick it up."

"Maybe we ought to talk about something else or maybe I'll just take a nap."

For Spencer, the thought of anyone taking a nap riding to an execution was too laid back, and Spencer did not want to leave the issue without closure that Herald would or could appreciate from his new hire.

"I took your suggestion and read the McBride case. You really did a masterful job."

Herald took notice and seemed more interested now than sleepy.

"I knew you read it. I got a call the day you found that piece of evidence in the Compton case you are working on. At first, I was concerned that you were poking around in a place you shouldn't be, so I told the records clerk it was my idea. Did it help?" anticipating a positive answer.

"Sure did. You had a mastery of the crime scene. Every detail accounted for, almost like being a detective on the scene."

"Well, that came from looking at and listening to the pictures. As long as you have a good photographer in the PD, you don't have to be there and run the risk of being called as a witness to the crime scene. That is something I have always avoided. I would hate to be conflicted out just because I was curious about a crime scene, but I know it happens and I know you guys are being called out to give on-scene advice on search warrants and evidence collection. Just remember, in a big case stay clear. OK?"

"I think we are all careful about that. I think I know what you mean about listening to the pictures and I like the way you put it. Where did that come from?" Spencer asked.

"Thanks. There was an old TV host on a national Sunday morning news show who always signed off by saying, 'See you on the radio'. It brought to mind that we watch a lot of TV and listen, but there is much more to it. He was trying to tell us to use our imagination beyond just listening, and the same applies to crime photos or any photos for that matter.

You and I haven't had a case together and we will. I hope you get the same experience my other assistants have had with photographic evidence. In one case I asked my assistant to review the photographs and he essentially told me what he thought they showed. The problem was he was not listening to the pictures. He just described them. The case involved an old man who was murdered at his front door early one morning. The killer came early and the old man carried a small aluminum baseball bat for protection as he answered the door. Regrettably, he didn't have time to use it, but the killer claimed the old man immediately attacked him with the bat for no reason and he was forced to defend himself by stabbing the old man. The bat was found on the floor next to the old man's body. My assistant told me that the problem with the case was that there was a bat the killer claimed he used in self-defense and it had blood on it.

The killer was not injured and the blood on the bat was never tested but was assumed to be the blood of the victim. I looked at the pictures of the bat and listened to them for what seemed like hours until the picture spoke to me. There was blood on the bat. No doubt about that and it formed two parallel streaks that ran from the top center down and around the side of the bat to where it dripped onto the floor. The blood did not run down the bat and the streaks were straight. I put the scene in action like a movie director and concluded that the bat had to be on the ground before the old man was stabbed. Can you see why?"

"Not sure without seeing the photographs," Spencer replied.

"No one else saw it either. Not the police and not my assistant who kicked himself when I pointed out the gravity of the situation. That's a pun. Get it?"

"I'm starting to," Spencer realized. "I'm thinking the clue is in gravity somehow and its effect on the bat or maybe the blood."

"Right on both points, but mostly the effect of gravity on the blood that ended up on the bat. The old man was known to carry the bat to the door whenever anyone came knocking. When he answered the door, he was immediately stabbed in the chest and he dropped the bat at his feet. By then blood started to flow and dripped straight down from the old man who was still standing. It hit the stationary bat and gravity carried it around – not down – the bat proving that the bat was not swung but was on the ground at the time the blood arrived on it. That picture told the whole story and the killer was convicted. Without listening to the pictures of the bat and the blood it would have been a murder versus self-defense against a crazy old man with a bat and maybe enough for reasonable doubt."

"That is a fascinating story," Spencer admitted. "I guess the moral of the story is to do the listening yourself and not just rely on the criminalist experts."

"None are perfect and, yes, they do miss important stuff. So, we have to do more than just look at the evidence. Listen to it."

"Lesson learned," Spencer said, but thinking that listening was really nothing more than horse sense that his father had given him as a steady diet.

"When you were looking at the McBride case was there anything that got your attention that is worth talking about?"

Spencer felt a sudden rush of adrenaline, and he hoped it didn't show by turning red in the face. How much did Herald know about what he was doing? Did he know what he was doing and how far should he go in answering that question. Evaluating his options with lightning speed, he decided that starting slow without much detail was the best approach. No sense in getting fired on the way to an execution by telling too much if it was not necessary. If Herald did know, he would just have to come clean and take his punishment. Spencer smiled thinking that if he got fired on the spot, Herald would be walking to Lucasville and Spencer would at least be driving home.

"Well, I have to admit that I didn't listen to the pictures like you do," Spencer began, "but there was enough graphic evidence to warrant the death penalty. What did you make of the blue nitrile glove that was found at the scene? It seems that the defense made a big deal out of it claiming that McBride had no reason to use gloves because he was there before and his prints were expected to be there."

"You read that I covered that, right? He left the glove to throw us off the track. Sometimes the simple answer is the best answer. Listen to that picture. What is it telling you? He planned to be there and planned to leave the glove. It was no accident or misstep of the killer. It was him and he planned it. Leaving the glove was proof of premeditation required at that time. Too bad the police didn't listen to the pictures or they would have had him confess to that too and saved a lot of questions. The DNA exam that came years later showed nothing on the glove except her blood. Those swabs of the glove ended that argument. I handled the transmittal of those personally to avoid a screw up."

"How embarrassing would it have been for you if someone else's DNA was found?" Spencer asked.

"Plenty, but it wasn't. I remember a lot of worry around that time, but I was always confident we had our man. For me, it's never a crap shoot, but I am a chance taker. I considered the risk and took the chance, not that I had any choice, and it worked out. Anything else?"

Again, Spencer wondered if Herald was probing so he continued on the path of an honest appraisal of the trial.

"I thought the police work on the confession was weak, if you don't mind me saying so. They had him for fourteen hours and promised him everything, except a pony and a free ride home if he would just confess. Unlike what we have now, there were no recordings, no video and nothing besides the word of the two detectives who grilled him unmercifully."

"Sounds like your old defense stripes are coming out."

"Not really. I am still critical of browbeating because it can evoke sympathy and is usually unnecessary. One of the first cases I had here was a case where the Sheriff's detective did the same thing without success, and I won the case after telling the jury how happy I was that the defendant didn't confess because they would not have believed it. I won on other evidence and not a questionable confession."

"I heard about that. The department was not too happy with you throwing the detective under the bus. I never mentioned it to you because you won the case. If you hadn't, it might have been a different story. You might want to consider that next time."

Those words encouraged Spencer to think there would be a next time. Herald didn't know or there would have been no veiled threat.

"Obviously, I still have a lot to learn and I am working my way through with your cases to get a good feel for how you do it."

"Well, don't try to copy anyone. You have your own style, but there are ways to expand on what you do. The prosecutor's office is the best place to do it because no one ever gets hurt. Victims always come to us injured. We can't change that win or lose. You take one of those capital defense attorneys. If they lose, their client dies. If a med-mal attorney loses, it's only money. If we lose, it's just 'next case'. See what I mean?" Herald said.

"After reading the testimony of McBride's mother, it's hard not to think of her as a victim too, and feel at least sorry for her loss. It's that human factor that's hard to shake."

"That's probably because she has attacked you from the day you started with her alibi claim, but it didn't stand up to cross examination. Remember, there are always victims on both sides."

"I agree. But what if you couldn't break her?"

"It was like taking candy from a baby. You talk about the human factor. I think the jury was more impressed with her just giving her son unconditional love to the point of lying and even then, she couldn't get her story straight. She couldn't remember anything about the day of the murder except she was exact about her memory of McBride being with her. A parrot could not have done as well. In the end it was just her and McBride. No chorus of witnesses on the alibi, just a duet by mother and son. Not convincing. You would think that with all the time and preparation before the trial that she would get it straight, but she didn't, and she made it easy for me. From what I hear, she has a hard time dealing with that."

"You might be right on that. At best she is simply pathetic. Kind of like a lost soul that we have to deal with."

Spencer wanted to add that she was also a constant reminder that he does have to work with humanity and that there are consequences that often cannot be avoided. Molly was one of those.

"Right again. Let me know when we get close," Herald said, signaling the end of the conversation and leaning into the corner of his seat to shut his eyes.

Spencer was disappointed in himself for never asking what to expect when they arrived at the institution. Herald would know. He probably had more experience with executions than any prosecutor in the state regardless of the size of the office. He decided the best course was to follow the leader, say nothing or as little as possible and take it all in. He noticed a car close behind and realized he was slowing down again, so he picked up the pace, but felt a desire to be not moving at all. Time would not stand still and wishing would not change anything.

Spencer could not help wondering what was happening with McBride as they drove through the countryside. It was a clear day. The sun was bright. The world seemed at peace. He knew that McBride was surrounded by concrete painted brick walls. No windows there and just uniformed attendants who probably made no eye contact or gave any non-scripted words. Perhaps there was a priest to give McBride some sense of encouragement that the end of his miserable wait was almost over. Was McBride in some unimaginable panic about what would happen shortly? It was thoughts of McBride's experience now that Spencer could not comprehend except in his own warped imagination. After years of denying Molly the opportunity to see him, was McBride now looking for her one last time or did he continue to deny her existence for her sake? Spencer would know by her absence, but he knew, if not, that she, too, was waiting in the shaded emptiness of her apartment for word of the end.

Chapter Twenty-Five

A mileage sign on the highway said "Lucasville 30 Miles" which matched his GPS, so he had about a half hour before things got busy. He would have to wake Herald to get final directions when they got to the institution. Spencer had put his phone on vibrate, and it went off which was not unusual for this time of the day. From the caller I.D. he could see it was Patterson from the crime lab, and he answered quickly and quietly without thinking about content so as not to wake Herald.

"Hello, Agent Patterson. I've been waiting for a call from you. Any word on the tests yet?"

"What the hell are you doing, Tallbridge?"

"Well, I am actually on my way to an execution. What are you doing?" Spencer said with a disarming attempt at humor.

"Maybe I'm on my way to one too. I really have to ask what you were thinking with the stuff you sent in."

Spencer felt another adrenaline rush like the one he had with Herald an hour earlier. "What do you mean?" Spencer asked without saying too much that Herald might hear, but knowing the answer.

"Don't give me that bullshit. You know exactly what I mean. You sent up the board. I get that. But then you added five more items and lied about where they came from. I can get fired over this. I'm really pissed and…"

Suddenly the call was dropped. Spencer was so far out in the country that cell phone service was either non-existent or blocked by the hills on the way to Lucasville. A county with a small population in the middle of nowhere was the perfect place for a penitentiary, but not so good for cell service. Spencer immediately tried to call back to explain as best he could without success. A realization hit Spencer that he had not only been caught for his good intentions but had ground so far into the quick that there was no way out except to get it all out. He was just about to wake Herald and come clean when his phone started to vibrate with another incoming call. It was Patterson again.

"Sorry. The call was dropped. I didn't hang up," Spencer quickly announced.

"I figured that, but you are really in a heap of trouble. I think I know what you're doing somehow but I don't know exactly what to make of it. I'm not sure I want to know. That cigarette butt had testable DNA and we don't know exactly who it's from directly, but we know its closest relative. I think you know, too, William McBride. He's the same guy that we examined a few years ago. It really wasn't much of a task in making the connection in our data base. You have the Compton case and just how do you think you are going to explain the submission probably of McBride's mother's or sister's DNA, if he has one, to the attorneys in that case? You somehow didn't think through whatever you're doing."

"Anything else?" Spencer asked, thinking he may as well get it all out about the remaining four swabs.

"Nothing of consequence. Oh yeah, there was DNA on the board from Mr. Compton, so I guess that helps. You were at least being honest about that. I was told that the McBride case was handled by your boss when I went through the results with my supervisor. Your boss must have been part of the scene investigation because the remaining four were all his that we've had on file for years just in case he ever touched something at a scene. You know the drill. I thought I was doing you a favor by trying to link up the unknowns and that's how you got found out."

The pause was so long that Patterson probably thought they were disconnected again, but he could hear the sound of the pavement like a heartbeat during the delay. Spencer could hear his own and he stayed with the call.

"What are you going to do about this, Tallbridge? I had to tell my supervisors. Sorry. I had no choice, not that I would have covered it up even if I could. But you have to know how much trouble you're in. This is really serious when you dummy up evidence and stick it in a case of someone else for testing. Nice try on asking for that separate report. We've never heard of this before, never. I shouldn't even be talking to you, but maybe there is a reason more than just being stupid. You used me and I am really pissed. I'm not sure if you ever got rid of those defense stripes and I think my supervisors are going to talk with your boss later today and recommend disciplinary action. He wants your ticket, your scalp and maybe even a criminal tampering charge. Are you getting all this? Where is he now?"

"In the car sitting right next to me asleep. I got this."

"You got this?" Patterson asked with surprised amazement. "How in hell do you 'got this'?" quoting the unimaginable response from Spencer.

"Yeah, I got this. I'll take it from here. Time to grind into the quick and there's no way out."

"What does that mean 'grind into the quick'?" Patterson wondered, sensing Spencer's awareness of how much trouble he was in and that it could end with disbarment.

"I'll be back with you later," Spencer said, without providing a definition and with an understandable tone of extreme seriousness. "You did what you had to do. Don't worry about me and please believe that no matter what you think of me and whatever happens next, thank you for doing your job. So long." Spencer hung up and powered off his phone. Lucasville and the end were now in sight and time to wake up Herald.

Spencer now felt older beyond his years. On one hand, a weight had been lifted with a level of clarity he never experienced before. He had eureka moments before in his career. They were moments of sudden enlightenment followed by euphoric inspiration, but nothing that compared with what he had now. How to play it was his primary concern with little time for anything other than instinctive and emerging decisions to make on the fly that he would have to trust. First, though, he had to wake up Herald.

"Mr. Herald, we're here."

"Thanks. I thought I heard you on the phone. Everything OK? Any last minute changes? Wow! Look at the crowd. Looks like a movie production site with all the cameras and satellite feeds. A lot more than last time. Must still be a go. Just continue on up to that first guard station to check in and get our passes."

Spencer passed on the "OK" question and did as instructed without mentioning anything about his conversation with Agent Patterson. When he arrived at the guard station the guard made the standard greeting and request.

"Good morning, gentlemen. Can I help you?"

Herald leaned over toward Spencer and answered with his prosecutor badge in hand.

"Good morning, officer. I am the Rutledge County Prosecutor Dan Herald along with my assistant prosecutor Spencer Tallbridge. We are here for the McBride matter."

"Yes, sir. I have you both on my list and I will need a picture I.D. from both of you." He gave no deference to Herald's badge.

Looking at Spencer, Herald asked seriously, "You did bring a picture I.D., didn't you?" as he handed his to the guard with a boarding house reach.

"Of course." Spencer brought out his driver's license and handed it over.

Once the identification process was completed, the guard handed two passes to Spencer and said they would have to be returned on their way out. The guard jokingly told them "No souvenirs" and directed Spencer how to proceed to the next station along the way to arrive at the place of the execution. Herald broke in and said he knew where it was and that nothing had changed since the last time he was there as if to tell the guard he was experienced beyond the regular traffic at these events.

As they arrived in the designated parking lot, Herald exclaimed, "I'll be damned. Looks like we have a full house. We're not late, are we?"

Spencer just shook his head. He instinctively knew what was coming. There was the Governor, the Attorney General and the Warden standing near the curb of the visitor's parking area as if waiting for Herald's arrival. Spencer believed they were waiting and not just for Herald.

"Good morning, Prosecutor Herald," the Attorney General began. "I think you have a problem."

"Don't tell me this is off again. I thought all possible delays were worked out last night."

"No," the Attorney General continued. "It's a problem with your assistant, Mr. Tollbridge, and my crime lab."

"Do you want to discuss that here?" Spencer broke in considering their less than formal location in an open parking lot for a matter with such grave circumstances. "And it's Spencer Tallbridge," he added assertively.

"I do, young man, because I think this is as far as you get today, but you might be back," he added. It was a veiled threat not immediately understood by Herald, the Governor or the Warden, but understood by Spencer. It was a possible criminal charge. For Spencer the time for talk was over. It would have to be the 80-yard Hail Mary pass to the end zone or nothing. With all the courage of his convictions he could muster, he began.

"Mr. Governor, I am an attorney, an assistant prosecutor and citizen of this state and as such I am hereby making a citizen's arrest of Prosecutor Dan Herald for the murder of Linda Stewart." With all formality he continued, "I hereby declare that William McBride is innocent of that crime and is wrongfully and unjustly held here today as he has for the past 27 years. Now would you like me to continue here or would you like to go inside. Your call because, if not, my next stop will be with the TV cameras out front."

"What is going on here?" the Governor asked. "Have you lost your mind?"

Herald broke in. "He must have. This is nuts. I am sorry, gentlemen. I don't know what's going on except for one thing for certain. Tallbridge, you're fired."

At that point the Attorney General joined in.

"Mr. Tallbridge, I heard you were coming today. I got a call from the Director of Investigations that you corrupted a case…"

Herald interrupted. "Not again." We've been here before. Tallbridge, what in hell did you do?"

The Attorney General continued. "I just need to know one thing. Where did you get the four samples of DNA you submitted to the lab and I need to know it now. Don't lie to me. Do you understand? I have a feeling where this might be going and I need to know now," he repeated.

"I do, sir," Spencer began. "The four samples that you heard about came…"

As Spencer summoned his courage of explanation, a guard in formal coat and tie walked up and announced to the Warden, "Sir, everyone is assembled and about to begin. I can have a secure line here for the Governor if you just…"

The Attorney General interrupted and barked an order telling the guard to put a hold on everything. "Don't make a mistake on this. Put everything on hold. We'll follow up shortly. Now get on with it, Tollbridge or Tallbridge, or whatever the hell your name is. Give me a straight answer." As the suited guard walked away, he called to stop the execution of William McBride. Spencer picked up where he left off. "I got the samples from inside four fingers of a glove found at the crime scene. It was photographed by the first responders and Herald was not one of them. He was never on the scene and he told me so. Presumably, the glove was examined years ago with no results. It's a long story, but I have been trying to convince McBride's mother of his guilt and that his conviction was not her fault and guessed, just guessed, that the inside of the fingers had never been tested. If McBride's DNA was in the glove, case closed, he's executed, and Mrs. McBride would have to understand. If nothing, case also closed at least for me and McBride's executed today. If it was someone else's, case open and McBride goes free or at least he gets a new trial. I would probably get fired, but not criminally charged. I never dreamed it would be Herald's DNA. So here we are."

"You son-of-a-bitch. You can't prove I killed her," Herald said. "My DNA doesn't prove I killed her. You've got nothing. Do you know what you are doing here to the death penalty? You're killing it. I'm leaving. I've had enough of this." He started to walk away and then stopped. Looking around, he realized there was no place to go. He was in one of the most secure prisons in the State of Ohio and he knew it. He had the sudden realization that he went at lightning speed from Prosecutor to being caught for murder and was now in a prison with more to come. His legs gave out and he sat on the curb with his head in his hands whimpering that this could not be happening. It was sensory overload beyond his comprehension having avoided discovery and getting away clean for decades.

"Dan, you said the magic words for me," the Attorney General said. "You said you can't prove it. You never said you didn't do it. For me and what this young man has given me, that's enough for now and as far as I'm concerned you are under arrest." The Attorney General continued with equally firm authority. "You have the right to remain silent. You have the right to an attorney. If you can't afford one, an attorney will be provided to you without cost. Anything you say now can and will be used in a court of law. Do you understand the rights I have given you?" Herald just looked up without responding. His mind had short circuited and had what detectives refer to as fractured brain syndrome. He could not put it all together. The Attorney General continued. "I just have one other question for you, Spencer, and I know the Governor will have a couple, but why did you only send the swabs of four fingers instead of all five? Seems like you were taking a pretty big risk there if the one needed was the one left behind."

"I was, sir. I needed to leave one finger pristine. I did think ahead of as many possibilities as I could. I actually thought that it was remotely possible that it would be someone else's DNA because of another case I heard about from a detective and I would have to convince Herald. With all he had invested in this case I didn't need a possible bus ride, if you know what I mean. With all that I was doing, I could not trust anyone and I had forsaken my oath to follow the law. For that I am sorry and I know there will be consequences. That's what happens when you grind into the quick."

"What does that mean, 'grind into the quick'?" the Governor asked as the Warden was making calls to have Herald taken into custody. Spencer said it just the way his father taught him about how far to go with anything worth going after and that bad things can happen, too, when things are taken too far.

With that the Governor said, "Well, gentlemen, where do we go from here? Just what am I supposed to tell the press now that we probably have an innocent man locked up we were about to execute? And besides the press is already playing up that McBride was willing to admit guilt again if I spared his life. I am open to suggestions. Mr. Tallbridge, you got us into this mess, and I would like you to give me some of your lawyerly advice. Maybe it's time for us to try that grind thing because I feel the grinder coming."

"Of course he would admit he killed her. He no doubt believes it's his last day, and he would have admitted that a monkey jumped out of his ass, if that would save him. They say you never think more clearly than the time just before walking up the stairs of the gallows and I suppose that was his last shot. All the same, I think there is a way out and a way to get out in front of this with a little horse sense even if it may be legally questionable. And by the way, not to alarm you more than you already have been, this might not be Herald's only one."

"Good Lord," the Governor said with exasperation. "I can't deal with any more now."

Just as Spencer was about to explain further, another guard approached the Warden with two others and told him that everyone was assembled and that they needed to get on with the execution or they would be off schedule for everything that follows an execution. If they were late there would be a delay in the process itself with the chemicals involved, the press release following the execution, the removal of the body and a number of other details that would be backed up.

"Didn't you get the message? Another example of governmental efficiency. Just tell them there will be delays – everything is on hold. Am I clear?" the Warden ordered. "I guess they didn't take the Attorney General's word for it," he said, "and take that man (pointing to Herald) to my office for now. He's in custody, but I don't want anyone to see that for the time being. When you get him there cuff him to a table cuff link and watch him close. I don't need a suicide today with everything else. No questions and he gets no calls. Pat him down and be sure to secure his cell phone, if he has one. Avoid anyone involved in the execution, the press, witnesses, anyone. Understand?" There was no need for a reply. "Take the long way around if you have to and, again, he talks to no one until I say so. Again, make sure the execution is on hold and no explanations, not that you know any." They Warden knew at least that much would have to be done.

"It won't be a delay," Spencer interjected, taking control of the narrative. "Tell them that a news conference will be given in three hours and that everyone should just sit tight until then." With a nod from the Governor, the Warden singled out the guard that was pressing to get started and told him for the last time to make the announcement.

"As I was about to say, I think you have something historic here and if you want to capture the hearts and minds of the citizens of this state, try this on for size," Spencer said. "Mr. Governor, I don't need to tell you that you have extraordinary powers that are seldom used or known about. While not the case here, under certain circumstances, you can even declare martial law. Just give me two hours to make it back to Rutledge. I need that time to tell Mrs. McBride what has happened here, and I need you to give me custody of McBride to take along."

"You've got to be kidding," the Attorney General interrupted. "How are we supposed to do that? How does he go from death row and twenty steps to his execution to a car ride to visit his mother? You don't mind if I think this is all a little crazy. I guess facts can be stranger than fiction. Nobody could write this stuff," he said with conviction.

"Who's in charge?" Spencer answered with a question and the Governor said assertively, "I am." The Governor then couninued,"This is starting to play out like a Frank Capra movie and I think it has legs. Is there any legal reason I can't do this?" he asked the Attorney General.

"Unless you think I'm wrong," Spencer volunteered, "and want to continue the suffering of McBride's mother and the continued wrongful incarceration of McBride. Let me take him home. You can do that. You have that power and I expect now the Attorney General will back you up. Sure, it's a first here and probably the first time this has happened in history, but its time has come and you need to be with it or against it. The time is now to put him in my custody. I'll take responsibility as an attorney even if I'm no longer an assistant prosecutor and maybe along the way I can convince him to settle his wrongful imprisonment case for less than the value of the State Capital. Your choice," he said with a laugh. "I want to get him home to his mother, and I don't want any word of this 'til that is done. It will play well for you if you go along with this, and I think my opinion and everything I have done has been on point so far."

"It's your call, Governor," the Attorney General said. "He's right on your powers and I'm all in for whatever you want to do. Things can happen fast in Ohio and maybe that will be our best point when we discovered the truth today."

The Governor took a moment for another consideration. "You know, Tallbridge, your county is going to need a new prosecutor in a hurry, and you said there would be consequences for what you did. Maybe not the consequences you expect, but interested?"

"Sure. I can't think of a better way to get back on the good side with my friends at the State Lab."

"OK, I'll make your appointment in the morning as Acting Prosecutor until we get the Herald case over with and then I'll make it final. Good thing there is no statute of limitations on murder. I don't even know what your politics are, and I might be in a little trouble with my party if your persuasion is different, but at this point I really don't give a damn."

Without further debate or inquiry, the Governor set out the plan. He asked the Warden to take Spencer to the holding area to meet McBride and tell him what was happening. He told Spencer to give the Warden his car keys and that the Warden should put it where Spencer and McBride could leave without being noticed and ordered the Warden to take all necessary steps without delay to get Spencer and McBride on the road back to Rutledge. For their part, the Governor told the Attorney General to accompany him to the execution witness holding area to tell all in attendance that the execution simply would not go as planned and that a full statement and meeting with the witnesses would be conducted in the institution press area in three hours, giving Spencer plenty of time to get back to Rutledge County. Lastly, the Governor asked the Attorney General to take steps to get Dan Herald into the hands of law enforcement without letting on what transpired in advance of the press conference and to continue him on a suicide watch, a likely consideration for Herald given his new circumstances.

Chapter Twenty-six

Then the Warden cleared a path through multiple levels of security on the way to the execution holding cell where McBride was being held. When they finally arrived, McBride was sitting on a metal bench in a small concrete block cell with no windows. He was alone and looking down, only looking up when the Warden announced, "He's all yours."

"Is it time?" McBride asked. "Is my mom here? Are you another Chaplain?"

"Hello, Billy. I don't know how to tell you this, but let me just get it out," Spencer began slowly. Then, suddenly and fighting back tears born out of the pressure cooker he was living in that day and the sheer joy of the moment he announced, "You're going home. You and I, we're leaving and leaving now. Don't ask any questions. Just wait 'til we get to the car. Let's go."

"But..."

"No buts. Let's go, but don't worry. No one will change their minds. No one will stop us. We need to go now."

McBride arose almost robotically, anticipating how he would have reacted when he would have walked when ordered those last few feet to his death.

"Do I get handcuffed?" It was standard practice that anywhere he was ever escorted in the institution or to court hearings that he would have to be hand and ankle cuffed. He could not remember a time when he was out of his cell without them.

"No. Those days are over. No questions now, OK? We have to get out of here."

The Warden was waiting just outside the holding cell and reached out to McBride as he walked by. He took McBride's arm to hold him back for a moment and began.

"McBride. This has been one hell of a day. As long as I live there will never be another one like it. You didn't cheat death. This good man saved your life. You might ask him what it means to grind into the quick, but he did it for you and I am glad for you. What has happened to you over the years and today may well have changed history, and I am proud to be a part of it. Please accept my sincere apology for the lost years and everything else.

Good luck."

With that, the Warden again cleared a path and, when they got to an exit where Spencer's car was waiting, the Warden who had walked with them told one of his guards to give McBride his uniform coat and hat. "I need you to get those back to me, but no rush and I know you don't have a cent so here's everything I have on me," and handed McBride all the money he had in his pocket.

McBride now looked less like a convict and more like an employee. Spencer began the winding drive down to the front gate of the institution passing a funeral home hearse in the opposite direction to where he was once again met by a security force. This time, however, the guard, on his cell phone with the Warden, just looked in and waved the pair through with nothing said except, "I just need your pass Mr. Tallbridge," which Spencer gave him with a smile. As Spencer and McBride passed near the death watch of the press, Spencer told McBride not to look up and keep his head down. There were also protesters everywhere holding signs and pictures of McBride, but not one considered that the pair leaving had anything to do with an execution. Spencer took note of the irony that several protesters, thinking McBride was a guard, cursed him unmercifully as a murderer as they passed.

"Where have I heard that before?" Spencer thought to himself with a smile and relief that he may never have to hear those words again.

As they left the penitentiary in the rear-view mirror, neither Spencer nor McBride could bring them to start talking. In a way, it was easier for McBride. Most of his adult life was spent in silence. Spencer turned on the radio and tuned it to an oldies station that was playing "In Dreams" by Roy Orbison. That was all it took to get the tears to start flowing from McBride. First, just a few and then a river that he could not control or stop. Spencer knew instinctively no words would change that, and he just had to ride it out literally and figuratively. Spencer decided to take the opportunity to make a call to Dog by the Pound.

"Hello, Janet. This is Spencer Tallbridge. Remember me?"

"I do. Finally decided you need a dog after all?" she hoped.

"It's not for me, but I do need one of those yellow lab pups, if you still have any."

"I do. There has been a lot of interest. There always is with lab pups. When do you want to stop by?"

"In about an hour with any luck. I'll need some sort of a box or cage or something. Credit card OK?"

"Sure, but if you want to pay later in cash, I trust you. After all, if I can't trust you as a prosecutor, who can I trust? I'll have a travel case for you. You can borrow it until things get set up."

The irony of the question of trust was not lost on Spencer, but he still acknowledged, "I appreciate your trust."

"Is anything wrong? I hear crying in the background. Did someone just lose a dog? You didn't hit one with your car, did you? I get those calls."

"No. I am taking a friend to visit his mother who's not well and neither is he, I think. It will be all right and the dog will help. I'm sure of it. Man's best friend. Right?"

"Right. I told you that you should get one, too. We'll be ready for you. See you soon. Bye."

After a few more miles, McBride finally got hold of himself and started to talk and question the most bewildering events of the day in his otherwise monotonous life in prison.

"You know I'm supposed to be dead now," McBride began. "I am not supposed to be here. How is it possible that I am here? You always hear about people wondering if things were really happening. You know, the pinch me thing. That never happened to me except when I was convicted. I thought it was just a nightmare. I forced myself to sleep hoping that I would wake up and it would all be just a bad dream. But it wasn't a dream. Have you ever had those kinds of dreams where everything is so real until you wake up? I always hoped that was what was happening, but soon I knew it was over for me. I would never get out of prison and probably not by natural causes anyway. Sleep and dreams are no help. They really make it worse. Every time I wake up it starts over that I have to believe it is happening and that I am going to be killed for no reason."

"I think sleep will be better now. It might take some time and it will be all good when you wake up. You have to trust me on that."

"I don't even know who you are. I don't know what is going on. Did I win some kind of appeal? Are you a new lawyer for me? Could you just tell me what happened?"

"I think it's about time now and I hope you are ready for this. My name is Spencer Tallbridge and I am an Assistant Rutledge County Prosecutor. At least I was until about an hour ago when I got fired, but that's a whole other story. I got fired because I had some tests done on the evidence in your case. Are you following me so far?"

"I think so. You're a lawyer, but not my lawyer. Right?"

"Right. Anyway, I slipped the evidence for testing into another case to see if it matched your DNA. If it did, you would be dead now. It didn't, so you're not. The hooker is that it matched the DNA of my boss, Dan Herald, who prosecuted you. I just found this out today when it was discovered by the lab that I put that evidence into another case for testing. Bright idea that would have got me fired and probably prosecuted and disbarred. Still following?"

"Yes, but why would you do that for me? I don't even know you. I never heard of you and what was it about the evidence that only you saw and no one else saw over all these years?"

"It wasn't for you. It was for your mother who has for years called everyone in the prosecutor's office murderers and I didn't like it. I really just wanted to prove you guilty and deserving of the death you were about to get today. I never saw this coming. There might have been a fleeting thought of 'what if' but I always thought I would firm up your conviction and sentence. Your mother's a saint. She never gave up on you. Worst of all, she blames herself because of her testimony at trial that ended up getting you convicted. That was the hook for me. Fortunately, she still smokes, and I was able to sneak out a little of her DNA on a fresh cigarette butt when I dropped by for a visit. She smokes and has no friends. No visitors except for me. I had to wait 'til she smoked a cigarette and I had cigarettes. That visit also almost got me fired, too, which would have killed this whole thing."

"I don't believe it. I mean I believe it, but I can't see all this happening. Are you telling me that your boss killed Linda Stewart and framed me?"

"That's exactly what I'm telling you. I know it's hard to believe, but look at it this way. There were a lot of ways this could get screwed up and didn't. Was it luck? Probably. And in the end, it has been the perfect storm. So many things had to come together today. Not tomorrow or the next, but today. I guess it's like hitting the lottery and, fella, you hit it big time. That's about all I can say for now. There will be more to come about Herald. I'm not through with him yet and neither is the Attorney General, but that's not your concern. Get the picture now?"

"It's hard to take it all in. I am still not convinced this is not some sort of dream in a car with a guy I don't even know who keeps slowing down."

"Sorry. I do that when I talk too or think too much and try to drive, but you deserve answers and as many as I can give you for now. Yes, you are awake and no, this is not a dream. Hopefully, I won't cause an accident to prove it," Spencer laughed to lighten up the conversation and picked up the pace. "What I am doing now is again as much for your mom as it is for you. We need to get to her as quickly as possible because she is probably in the dark about the execution delay. Everyone thinks it is either just delayed or just put on temporary hold. She doesn't need that, but I want to pick up something for her and you. Something for both of you to care for and help both of you through what will be a tough adjustment."

"You're giving her a dog? Why are you giving her a dog?" realizing that the conversation with Janet at Dog by the Pound was about a dog for his mother.

"You weren't listening, were you? You both need a friend. Everyone tells me I need a dog because I don't have any friends, at least any that I can count on around here. I was thinking of getting a dog when I visited your mother. She likes dogs and would like one. She told me so. She really has never wanted much except to get even with prosecutors, so a dog was always out of the question. I think a dog will help you both. Do it for me, OK? And besides, it will get you both out of that third-floor apartment of hers, even if I have to pay for it. It won't be long before you can handle that."

"Whatever you say, but just how are we supposed to support a dog now? I don't have a dime except for what the Warden gave me, and I don't even know how much he did give me," as he pulled out two twenties, a five and eight singles.

"You have no idea what you are in for. You have been wrongfully imprisoned for twenty-seven years on a bogus charge dreamed up by a corrupt government official, the prosecutor, and nearly executed by the State of Ohio. Under Ohio law you have hit the Locked-Up Lottery and it's worth millions."

"I can't even think about that, but how many millions?" he asked with a smile.

"Lots," Spencer said with a chuckle.

"I really don't care. I would like my mother to have a better life. Can you handle all that?"

"No. It looks like I might be the next Prosecutor of Rutledge County and tomorrow I will at least be the Acting Prosecutor. It would be a conflict of interest. That means it would be unethical for me to represent you, but believe me, you will have plenty of representation and I'll keep an eye on you."

"With all you did, all the rules you broke, sounds like now you got religion," he remarked with a laugh.

"Well, I think I always had it. I just couldn't find it for a while, fortunately for you and me, too."

It suddenly hit Spencer about all that happened and could have happened to derail where he and McBride were at that moment. He thought to himself of all the things that brought them to where he they were, beginning with being born. He considered all the choices he made to advance in life that could have been different. Law school, yes, but he could have become an accountant. McBride would be dead. The choice to become a trial lawyer and eventually work for Herald, if not, McBride would be dead. He could have turned Molly away and dismissed her as just another courthouse loon with a mental problem. McBride would be dead. He might not have been assigned the Compton case to eventually corrupt it with samples from the McBride case. McBride would be dead. And finally, Patterson may not have placed the call before the execution. McBride would be dead. McBride broke the silence.

"You're slowing down again."

"Sorry, when I first met you in the holding cell you asked me if your mom was there. She told me that she never visited you because you didn't want her to. You told her to forget about you. If you don't mind, tell me why you thought she might be there to see you die?" It was not a good question and not the right time. It was still too close to the time of the planned execution and McBride started to cry again without answering. The crying did not stop for 15 miles, and then he began choking out the answer through his tears.

"My life was over when I was sent to prison. My lawyers told me that the best they could hope for was delay or an end to the death penalty, but no way going home. I always knew I was innocent and so did mom, but nothing would ever change where I was and where I would eventually die, even if it was by old age. I thought about my horrible life every day and knew my mother did, too. I couldn't stand the pain of her suffering thinking about me. If she could just forget about me or if I could just kill myself, her life would be better. On death row there is no way to kill yourself unless you're real clever and I'm not clever. That's why I confessed. I actually thought that I would be able to go home. That's how stupid I was. So, I told her to get out of my life. It would be best for both of us."

"I get all that. I read your confession, but why ask if she was there?" hoping that he now had better control of his overwhelmed emotions.

McBride began deliberately and calmly. "When you are in that holding cell and there is nothing left to say or hear, you just wait for the Warden. You know he is coming and so is the end. The Chaplain is done with you. The lawyers all say their goodbyes and tell you how hard they worked to save you. The Warden was last on the list and you only sit there staring at the pattern of the painted concrete blocks in front of you while waiting for him. At that moment when you walked in, I had just one wish. Maybe just call it a feeling of hope that I might get to see my…" His voice cracked and the tears flowed again for another fifteen miles or so, maybe more, and Spencer got the point. Even at the very end when everything has been taken away, humans can still have hope for something good and pure in those last moments which his mother surely was on both counts.

"I think I understand. You always hear that a dying soldier calls out for his mother on the battlefield and you were about that close."

"You thought I was guilty all along, didn't you?"

"I did. I thought about a few impossible possibilities that I quickly dismissed. Even from the standpoint of being a former defense attorney in my other life, I thought you were guilty and deserved what you got."

"So, you believe in the death penalty?"

"I did. Not anymore. I had an epiphany."

"What's an efany?" Billy asked awkwardly.

"Sorry. It's just a big word that means a sudden awakening like you probably had when you realized finally today that this was not a dream and was really happening."

"Why does my case make a difference since I'm not guilty? Wouldn't you still want me dead, if I did it?"

"Well, my sudden awakening has nothing to do with the legal concepts of guilt and the equal and unequal application of executions, its cost and value as a deterrent that Herald always claimed. It has everything to do with my understanding for the first time that execution is not punishment. It is just elimination and that's the epiphany I've had in all this. If you were guilty, would I personally want you dead? Of course. That's not punishment. That's just vengeance that always gets confused with justice. I know now it's the same thing. It's just vengeance masquerading as a good word we call justice. It might make me feel good about killing you or the state killing you, but it's not punishment. How can it be punishment, if it happens in an instant like the electric chair, hanging or all the other quick methods? Or by just putting someone to sleep like that dog you had as a kid?"

"Mom told you about Sport, did she?"

"Yes, and it got me thinking today. That dog went down with love not hate, but still went down. That was no penalty and was merciful. The point is that the word 'execution' sounds good to those seeking justice, but in the end it's just an end. It's vengeance by elimination and that's not justice even if that's what you call it to make it sound good. And it doesn't matter how long it takes. It's all the same regardless how long you're on death row.

You've waited to be executed for almost 27 years and that had to be torture, and certainly punishment. That alone is punishment for someone who commits horrible crimes. It's not punishment if it happens quick like in Texas. I'm just taking the 'deserve to die' thing out of the justice thing, if you understand what I'm trying to say."

"I think so. You all wanted to string me up, but that's not punishment for me. It's just erasing me. Is that it?"

"That's pretty much it. There are many other arguments for really smart people to think about in opposition to the sentence, like what if the person is innocent or whether or not the sentence is fairly applied between races of people and between states that have it and those that don't. Those are what are called intellectual arguments that judges and politicians think about. Some folks argue that it costs too much to execute someone with all the appeals and court appointed lawyers. For me, with all that's happened today, it boils down to this. If I take away your car because you stole one, that's punishment. If I take away your life because you took another's, I am the only one who knows it; not you. You're dead. What I'm talking about is a new reality for everyday people or at least a reality that most people never think about now. I think they will after the world hears about this case, so you'd better be ready."

"Ready for what?" Billy asked.

"Ready to be the poster boy for the end of the so-called death penalty in America. That's what. People will come to know that taking away liberty permanently is a just punishment and death is nothing except for those seeking vengeance."

"Why did Herald do this to me and what happens to him now? Isn't he going to be another kind of poster boy, too?"

"His politics had a lot to do with it and what he is made of. You were just convenient. There will be a shit storm over this. Every prosecutor in the nation will be watching and shaking their heads. There will be an outcry to kill him, too. That's when the fun starts and you will take center stage, if you can or even want to. In this country there will be plenty of room for two poster boys."

"Twenty-seven years for being convenient," Billy said with resignation that nothing could return those lost years of his life. "I'll do my part. You can count on it."

"I am."

When they arrived at Rutledge, Spencer asked McBride if he wanted something to eat. They could stop at a fast food, but McBride jokingly said he already had a big last supper the night before. Spencer also had no appetite and went directly to Dog by the Pound where Janet had everything waiting for him. He thought it best if he just left McBride in the car because his face was probably on the news and Spencer could not bear the thought of another explanation or getting shot for helping an escaped convict.

"Here I am, Janet. Good to see you again. Here's my credit card and I hope you don't mind, but I am in a hurry and need to do this as fast as possible."

"Sure. No problem. The little guy has had all his shots and you need to take him back to the vet in six months for other stuff."

"Well it won't be me, but I'll make sure of it. Give me one of those 20-pound bags of puppy chow, too."

"He's had a lot of attention here and I know he will cry for a few days and nights. Tell the new owner to ignore it and it will get better. I promise."

"I think I get the crying part," he said cryptically. "I think the new owner will be shedding a few tears of love, too, so it will all work out."

Janet packed up the lab in his carrying case that had no name yet except "the little guy" and Spencer was curious about what Molly would name him. "It had better not be Spencer," he thought to himself as he left Janet's shop with arms full of puppy and puppy chow.

Spencer and McBride were now minutes away and McBride was taking in all the changes in the area.

"Didn't know things had changed this much," he said.

"I suppose time has stood still for you."

"Not so much considering my age. That has changed. Do you think my mother will recognize me?" he asked.

"I have no doubt about it. I just don't want it to be too much of a shock for her. When we get to her place, I want you to give me a few moments to wrap her brain around this. Hopefully the Governor hasn't let out the story yet. I guess we'll find out when we get to your mother's." He looked at his watch and saw that he was still within the time frame of their agreement.

As Spencer pulled into the parking area of Molly's apartment, he tuned his car radio to a local news station to hear if there was any news coverage. The commentator announced, "Breaking news. The execution of William McBride is delayed again. The Governor is expected to speak to the press along with the Ohio Attorney General at any time. Stand by for a detailed report."

When Spencer and McBride arrived at Molly's door, Spencer knocked loudly. After a short wait, he knocked again. Suddenly, Molly answered by saying, "Leave me alone. I told you I don't want to talk to you. Go away. Just go away. I told you I have no comment."

"It's me, Molly, Spencer Tallbridge. I need to talk to you. Please open the door."

"Why would I ever want to talk to you? I told those news people I have nothing to say and I mean it."

"Look, Molly, I'm going to be in a lot of trouble, if you don't open the door. I promise it will only take a minute. I have something I have to give you."

Spencer heard the door unlock and the door was slowly opened as Molly turned away with her back to Spencer expecting him to enter. McBride stayed behind holding the puppy he took out of its cage and was squirming to get loose. He rested his back on the wall next to the entrance waiting for Spencer to tell him to come in.

"I heard from the news people you haven't murdered Billy yet. I can't stand this. I can't stand this," she repeated.

"I want you to sit down. Please sit down. I am afraid you might fall down. Oh, what the hell, Billy come in here," he ordered.

As Billy came through the door, Molly saw him and dropped to her knees. She started to faint forward, and Spencer quickly went to his knees and caught her before she went face down. She was gasping for air and could not speak as Spencer lifted her up. Looking up, her eyes told that she questioned in disbelief that she was indeed seeing that Billy was home.

"Is it true? Spencer, what is happening?" Her voice was shaking and nearly inaudible, but Spencer could hear and steadied her shoulders.

"It's true, Molly. It's over. Your son has come home and home to stay. And he brought you something I want you to have."

Billy now came close to Molly and steadied her. As he did, she hugged him instantly with a grasp that would test the strength of anyone that might try to pull them apart. And the pup was there, too, yipping all the time.

"What's this?" she asked through a mix of a laughs and tears.

"Man's best friend, Molly," Spencer said as Billy and Molly joined with laughs and tears. "Just don't name him Spencer."

"There's a lot to tell and we have plenty of time now, but first I have to make a call and you just might want to start watching TV again," as he pulled out his cell phone and dialed a number.

"Hello, Arnold. This is Spencer Tallbridge. Are you ready for your full report?"

The End

Look for more books from Winged Hussar Publishing, LLC – E-books, paperbacks and Limited Edition hardcovers. The best in history, science fiction and fantasy at:

https://www. wingedhussarpublishing.com

or follow us on Facebook at:

Winged Hussar Publishing LLC

Or on twitter at:

WingHusPubLLC

For information and upcoming publications

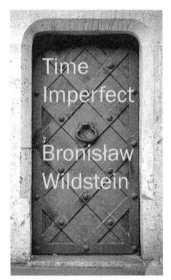

Section 130

Katrinka Manderly

About the Author

Michael T. Gmoser is a graduate of Miami University at Oxford, Ohio and Chase College of Law. He served as Criminal Division Chief of the Butler County Prosecutor's Office from 1974 to 1982 and left to pursue a trial practice in both criminal and medical negligence law. He was appointed the Butler County Prosecuting Attorney in February, 2011 to fill an unexpired term and was elected Prosecutor November, 2012 and re-elected in 2016.

In March 2011, Prosecutor Gmoser was awarded the James S. Irwin Professionalism Award "for his dedicated work in the legal profession and to our community as an attorney and community leader." Among many other activities, and a close second to his work as Prosecutor, he considers his service on the Butler County Certified Ethics and Grievance Committee for 36 years and Co-Chairmanship for 8 years to be the most significant and rewarding.

Most recently, Prosecutor Gmoser was appointed by the Ohio Prosecuting Attorney's Association to the Legislative and Executive Committees of that organization. He also carries an AV Martindale-Hubbell rating which is the highest rating for excellence by that nationally recognized rating service.